PERIL IN PAXTON PARK

A PAXTON PARK COZY MYSTERY BOOK 1

J. A. WHITING

To hear about new books and book sales, please sign up for my mailing list at:

www.jawhitingbooks.com

❀ Created with Vellum

For my family with love

CONTENTS

Chapter 1	1
Chapter 2	11
Chapter 3	21
Chapter 4	29
Chapter 5	39
Chapter 6	49
Chapter 7	59
Chapter 8	69
Chapter 9	79
Chapter 10	89
Chapter 11	101
Chapter 12	111
Chapter 13	121
Chapter 14	129
Chapter 15	139
Chapter 16	149
Chapter 17	161
Chapter 18	169
Chapter 19	177
Chapter 20	185
Chapter 21	195
Chapter 22	205
Chapter 23	213
Chapter 24	219
Thank you for reading!	227
Books By J.A. Whiting	229
About the Author	231

1

Twenty-eight-year-old Shelly Taylor stood on the deck of the Paxton Park Diner at the base of Park Mountain soaking up the sun's afternoon rays. She let her eyes wander over the pine forest, the bright blue lake spreading out towards the woods, the people returning from a hike, others launching canoes and kayaks, and a few taking a dip in the chilly water.

Shelly let out a long, deep, contented breath. She'd only been in Paxton Park for two weeks, but she was beginning to feel settled and comfortable and enjoyed the many outdoor activities available to her in the area.

A warm breeze caused some strands of her long, light brown hair to flutter over her forehead into her eyes and she pushed them aside as she gazed up at some of the mountain trails. In the winter, the resort burst with skiers and snow boarders, and in spring, summer, and fall, people flocked to the area for white-water rafting, mountain biking, hiking, and swimming.

At first, Shelly hesitated when she was offered the part-time position of baker for the diner and the on-site bakery, but now that she'd been working for a couple of weeks, she was happy with her decision to make a change and try something new and looked forward to experiencing the different seasons of Paxton Park, Massachusetts.

A man with salt and pepper hair poked his head out of the diner's door. "The timer went off in the kitchen, Shelly."

"Thanks, Henry." Shelly headed inside walking across the deck with a slight limp to her right leg. A car accident of six months ago resulted in her leg broken in two places, a punctured lung, four broken ribs, and a fractured collarbone.

Shelly didn't remember much about the crash except the terrible, unearthly sound of metal twisting and glass shattering as if the car was trying to slash a hole from this world into another universe. She'd spent a long time in the hospital, in rehab, and in out-patient physical therapy.

A talented baker, Shelly had been set to buy a small bakery in Boston after scrimping and saving for several years, but lost out on it when she ended up hospitalized for so long. It turned out that having the money in the bank was a stroke of good luck since she needed it to live on after the accident. The orthopedic doctor told her she was lucky to have walked away from the destroyed vehicle, and it was true, the driver and another passenger in the car had died that day, along with part of Shelly's heart.

"It sure smells good in here." The big, meaty man in his late sixties held the door open for the young woman to enter. "Any chance there might be an extra cookie or two in this batch?" Henry rented the diner from the mountain resort's owner and in addition to running the place, he worked as the cook.

Shelly grinned. "I think there might be."

There was a large, well-equipped kitchen located between the diner and the Mountain Bakery and Shelly worked creating baked goods for both places. There was a huge grill located next to the wall on the diner side. The wall had a cut-out in it so that orders could be passed through the window and plates of food could be set on the shelf for the waitresses to pick up. Henry enjoyed talking to the customers through the window from his position by the grill. The man and his wife, Melody, had been running the diner for over twenty years and for two different owners. Shelly and Henry hit it off right away and chatted and joked with one another as they went about their tasks which made the kitchen a warm, enjoyable place to work.

Shelly removed the last baking sheet from the oven with Henry practically drooling over her shoulder. "You might want to let these cool before you eat some."

"I can't wait." Henry took one of the chocolate-caramel cookies and bit into it. Practically moaning with pleasure, the man mumbled, "Heavenly." After eating a second one, he told Shelly, "You are the best baker I've ever met."

With a laugh, Shelly said, "The best baker is the one who happens to be in your kitchen." She made a cup of tea while waiting for the cookies to cool and sat down on a stool next to a stainless steel work table.

"Did you go to culinary school?" Henry asked as he removed clean dishes from the dishwasher and stacked them on the counter.

"No, I learned to bake from my grandmother. I majored in business and entrepreneurial studies in college. My Grandma said you can be a great baker, but in order to run a successful bakery, you need to study business."

"Good advice." Henry nodded.

"She was a smart cookie," Shelly joked. "How did you learn the business?"

"Trial and error. I never went to college, got a part-time job as a short-order cook while I was in high school and just kept at it." Henry carried the stacked plates to the cabinet. "I always wanted my own place, but Melody and I like Paxton Park and decided to stay here working at the resort." The man smiled. "Twenty years later and we're still here."

"I like the town, too." Shelly set her teacup down on the table and smiled. "Will I still be here twenty years from now?" She moved the cookies into a large metal container and snapped the lid on.

"You never know. The place kind of grows on you. Nice people, plenty to do, beautiful scenery, peaceful. You could do worse, that's for sure." Henry removed his apron. "Whaddya say? Shall we call it a day and lock up?"

"Sounds good."

The two stepped out onto the sunny deck.

"You have your bike or do you need a lift into town?" Henry asked.

"I have my bike, but thanks." Shelly slung her backpack over her shoulders and headed across the small gravel lot to the bicycle rack. "See you in the morning."

Riding away from the resort, Shelly followed the road for two miles to the main street of town which bustled with tourists and townspeople walking along the brick sidewalks. There were gift shops and clothing stores, pubs, restaurants, a small market, library, bookstore, and two inns. Flowers bloomed in pots and spilled over white picket fences. Shelly thought it was just about the prettiest town she'd ever seen.

Turning her bike down a side street lined with tall Maple trees and small well-tended cottages each painted a soft pastel color, she pedaled to her rented yellow bungalow with a covered front porch. Shelly walked her bicycle to the rear yard and parked it next to the shed, went inside to change into shorts and a t-shirt, poured a glass of lemonade, and carried it out to the porch. She slid onto one of the white rocking chairs, set her drink down, and rubbed at her aching calf. Her leg sometimes throbbed from standing most of the day and she hoped over time, the pain would lessen. A warm, light breeze fluttered over her skin and the gentle rocking motion of her chair soon had her nodding off and in a few minutes, she slipped into sleep.

Ever since the accident, Shelly hadn't been able to sleep more than five hours a night. A doctor at the hospital told her that it wasn't unusual for different patterns to form after such trauma and that she would eventually get used to the new normal.

She hadn't shared with him that the reason for her short periods of slumber wasn't physical discomfort, it was the dreams. Nightmares plagued her almost every night, and if it wasn't a nightmare, it was an odd jumble of things that didn't seem to go together and left her feeling anxious and uneasy.

Since moving to Paxton Park, a new twist on the dreams had developed. Her twin sister, Lauren, appeared to her every time she slumbered and despite her longing for her sister, seeing Lauren in her nighttime visions left Shelly feeling confused, forlorn, and distressed. She often had the sensation that her sister wanted her to do something important, but she had no idea what it was, and then she'd wake with a start and, unable to fall back to sleep, would have to spend hours pacing around her cottage.

Naps were no exception and after Shelly drifted off to sleep in her rocking chair, she dreamt of swimming in the clear, blue water of the resort lake. In no time, her peaceful mood and slow, steady strokes gave way to a frantic feeling and her arms moved faster and faster through the water as her heart pounded with fear. Shelly pushed herself out of the lake on the opposite bank, and hearing her sister call for her, she raced through the woods to the trails and followed one of them up the side of the mountain.

Breathing hard, Shelly ran and ran trying to find Lauren in the forest. Just as she was about to give up and with tears running down her cheeks, she followed the bend in the trail and found her sister.

Lauren stood on the other side of a small pond. Her facial expression was tight and drawn and her gaze was trained on the edge of the water. When she looked up at Shelly, her sad eyes held her sister's. Slowly, Lauren lifted her hand and pointed.

Shelly couldn't see what her sister had gestured to so she moved her feet slowly over the ground to get closer to the pond. Her heart beat so fast and loud that it pounded in her ears and beads of sweat dribbled down her back.

A flash of anxiety rushed through Shelly's veins when she reached the slope of the bank and she stopped short. A body ... someone ... a young woman, her long black hair floating around her head, lay face up in the reeds.

The woman was dead.

Shelly bolted straight up in her rocker, glancing around, disoriented. *A dream. That's all it was.* She sucked in deep breaths and rested back in the chair. Her t-shirt stuck to her and she felt cold and clammy. Reaching for her glass of lemonade, she held it to her temple.

Someone walked up the sidewalk on the other side of the road and Shelly glanced over to look. As her eyes widened in surprise and her hand started to shake, the glass slipped from her grasp and hit the porch floor, the liquid splashing and the ice cubes scurrying over the wood.

The young woman hurrying to Main Street looked just like the dead girl in Shelly's dream.

About to stand up to follow after the dark-haired woman, a voice called to her from the side of the porch causing Shelly to yip in surprise.

"Oh, sorry." A smiling young woman with long, wavy, brown hair walked up onto the porch carrying a pie. She looked to be in her late twenties and was slim and fit.

"I was napping and just woke up." Shelly rubbed at her forehead trying to clear her head. "I didn't hear you walk up." She stood to greet the visitor.

"I'm Juliet Landers. I live next door." Juliet pointed to the pale blue cottage and then extended her hand to shake with Shelly. "I was away until yesterday. I saw that you'd moved in so I baked you a pie. I hope you like apple."

Shelly accepted the pie from her neighbor with a smile. "I love apple. That was really nice of you. Thanks so much. Why don't you stay for tea and we can have a slice of the pie?"

Shelly made tea and she and her neighbor settled at the small, circular, metal table on the porch. "Are you working at the resort?" Juliet asked.

"I'm a baker." Shelly poured the tea into delicate porcelain cups. "I'm baking for the diner and the bakery."

"Oh, no," Juliet frowned. "You're a baker? You'll hate my pie. I'm not exactly a good cook."

Shelly chuckled. "No worries. I'm sure it's delicious." She cut two slices and placed them on small, white plates and after taking a bite, she smiled. "It *is* delicious."

"You're being nice," Juliet said. "I have a very small repertoire of things I can make. They're edible and they won't poison you, at least."

The word *poison* made Shelly shiver for a second. "Do you work at the resort, too?"

Juliet nodded and wiped her lips with a napkin. "I've worked there for six years in different jobs. I started as a ticket seller, moved to kids' ski instructor, now in the winters, I teach adults snowboarding and skiing and I'm on the ski patrol. In the other seasons,

I do canoe and kayak tours, take people on the white water rafting expeditions, and do bike trail tours around the area."

Shelly's eyes widened. "No wonder you're so fit."

"I love to be outside." Juliet shrugged.

The two chatted about where they grew up, what they studied in school, and how they ended up in Paxton Park. Juliet said, "My family lives in Boston so this location was perfect for me. I can take the train into the city and it only takes about two and half hours to get there."

Shelly said, "I wanted a change from living in the city and someone I used to work with knew about the opening at the resort and suggested I apply." She sipped her tea. "I liked that the job was only four days a week to start." She mentioned the car accident and how she still needed to recover some physical skills, but glossed over the details of the incident. "So far, so good. I'm glad the job worked out. I like to hike, bike, and swim so this place is ideal."

"I should take you on a tour of the trails on the weekend," Juliet said. "There's this really interesting part of the woods. It's called the Crooked Tree Forest. Have you heard about it?"

"No," Shelly shook her head. "What is it?"

"It's a good-sized grove of trees on the south side of the mountain," Juliet said. "The pine trees have all grown in a weird shape. The trunks come out of the ground and then they bend, a lot of them at ninety degree angles, then they shoot out between four to nine feet parallel to the ground, and then grow upright again. Like I said, it's weird. I've never seen anything like it."

Goosebumps formed over Shelly's arms. "What caused them to grow like that?"

"There are a number of theories. A genetic mutation, weather caused it, people who lived in the area purposely bent the trees to use the wood for canoes, nothing's been proved though." Juliet leaned forward, the corners of her mouth turning up. "Then there are the other theories, like pagan rituals caused them to bend, fairies did it, witches or elves bent the trees, aliens did it."

Shelly chuckled. "I vote for aliens being responsible."

"Me, too." Juliet laughed. "Anyway, the place is popular with the tourists and the townspeople are very protective of the trees."

The young women made plans to hike some trails on Saturday morning and make a visit to the Crooked Tree Forest.

"Any other strange things about the town?" Shelly kidded.

"The usual assortment of people, some grumps, some full of themselves, lots of fun, nice people." Juliet lifted the last piece of pie to her mouth. "And then, of course, there's that murder."

Shelly's eyes bugged and she almost dropped her fork. "What murder?"

Juliet eyed Shelly. "You didn't hear about it?"

"No." Shelly sat straight. "When did it happen? No one mentioned it to me."

Juliet's face was serious. "It happened two months ago. A woman was found dead, not too far from the crooked tree grove. She'd been strangled."

Shelly's heart pounded as she recalled hearing something about a murder in the western part of the state. She wondered if she'd seen a news report with a picture of the woman and that was the reason she dreamt of a dead girl in the woods. "Who was she?"

"She'd only lived here for about two months. She worked in town, at Chet's specialty market. Her name was Meg Stores."

"How old was she?

"Twenty-nine."

"Are there suspects?"

"Not to anyone's knowledge." Juliet gave a shrug.

"The story has fallen out of the news. The police have come up dry." Narrowing her eyes, she looked at Shelly. "The town manager and the town selectmen would prefer the story take a low profile. They don't want the murder to scare off the tourists."

Shelly groaned.

"My sister, Jay, is on the police force." Juliet added, "She keeps me up to date on things." Pointing at an angle to a cottage on the opposite side of the street located four houses down, Juliet said, "Meg lived in that pale pink house."

Shelly turned and leaned back so she could see which house it was. Her throat felt parched. She poured more tea into her cup and gulped it down. "What did she look like?"

"Sort of like us. Similar height and build, athletic, long hair ... darker though, almost black."

A shiver of nervousness ran down Shelly's back. "I thought I noticed a young woman who matched that description walking up the street right before you came over."

"Yeah, that's Meg's older sister, Maria. She came up when Meg was found and took her home for burial once the body was released. She returned recently to clear things out of the house. Maria isn't very friendly, but under the circumstances, it's understandable." Juliet shrugged a shoulder. "I offered to help her in any way I could. She declined. She told me to butt out, she said those very words. I keep my distance."

"How awful," Shelly muttered, taking another glance at the house where Meg used to live. "No one at the diner or bakery mentioned it."

"It was the only thing that anyone talked about for a month, then the subject faded away. At first, people seemed a little suspicious of each other, but then things went back to normal."

"Did the news of the murder impact the resort? Have tourists canceled their reservations?"

"A few did, not many though ... and a few days after the news broke, reservations actually increased." Juliet rolled her eyes. "I guess some people love murder mysteries."

"Are there any theories about what happened to the woman?"

"Not really. An idea floated around that someone she'd known might have followed her to town and killed her. Maybe a rejected boyfriend, someone who was angry with her over something. Nothing panned out."

"Did you know her at all?" Shelly asked, unease poking at her. A young woman, close in age to herself, had come to Paxton Park for a job and rented a cottage on the same street. The situation was too similar to her own.

"I introduced myself, but we never got together," Juliet said. "Our work schedules didn't mesh. I saw her in town a few times, we talked, nothing seemed to be out of the realm of normal." Juliet added, "I was out of town when it happened."

"How about the people who live on this street? Are most renters?"

"Only a few houses are rentals. The rest of us own." Juliet looked over at her house. "I rented my place when I first got here. After the second year, I approached the owner and asked if he wanted to sell. He did, so I bought it."

"Are you friendly with the other people who live here?" Shelly was feeling suspicious of the residents.

Juliet sipped her tea. "For the most part, the people are pleasant."

"Anyone you don't like?"

"Not really. Some don't say much, stick to themselves more."

"Did anyone else move in around the same time Meg Stores did?" Shelly couldn't shake the worry that the killer might be living on the same street.

"One guy. He lives at the end of the road. He does

maintenance at the mountain. I only know him to wave to." Juliet smiled. "Trying to figure out who did it?"

Shelly let her eyes wander over the houses. "Just wondering if there's anyone in particular I should be concerned about."

"Don't worry. If I hear anything, I'll be sure to warn you." Juliet followed Shelly's gaze out over the neighborhood. "I felt the same way when it happened. Everyone I saw, I wondered if he or she was the killer. I guess it's only natural. I didn't like the feeling that I couldn't trust the townspeople. The feeling has sort of waned." The young woman checked the time. "I'd better get going. It was nice chatting."

Shelly thanked Juliet for the pie and the two made arrangements to meet early Saturday morning to hike the mountain trails and visit the crooked trees.

"Take care." Juliet waved as she went down the porch steps and headed for her house.

A shiver of unease washed over Shelly as she wondered if moving to Paxton Park had been a huge mistake.

3

With the early morning light filtering through the leaves and tree limbs, Shelly and Juliet moved along one of the trails on the south side of the mountain. Some mist rose off of the lakes and the small meadows giving the wooded space a mysterious atmosphere. Juliet told Shelly some history of the area. "Western Massachusetts was originally settled by Native American societies like the Nipmucs, Mohawks, Mahicans and then English settlers made their way out here. The soil is good for farming and there are tons of rivers so the area was attractive to the settlers. Artists, musicians, and writers have flocked out this way and now the area is known for having a vibrant artist colony. A short drive away will bring you to Tanglewood, the famous music venue."

Juliet went on, "Park Mountain is part of the Berkshires and the Appalachian Mountain range and in the winter, the resort runs forty-eight ski trails. In the summer, along with the outdoor activities, we have the alpine super slide and the mountain coaster. Families love those. You need to try them, they're so much fun." Juliet laughed. "I sound like an advertisement playing on television."

"Well, if I hadn't already moved here, I'd jump on the train and head to Paxton Park." Shelly hadn't quite regained her stamina after the accident and needed to stop to catch her breath on the steep part of the trail. Juliet had taken her past beautiful clear lakes and streams, to a lookout trail with a fabulous view over the countryside, and to see the resort's windmills on the slope that generated power for the resort facilities.

"You okay?" Juliet looked back to where Shelly was leaning on a tree trunk. "Is your leg holding up?"

"I just need a little rest." Shelly smiled. "I'll be ready in a minute."

"We're almost to the flatter section of the trail." Juliet pulled her water bottle from her pack and took a long swig. "We can take a swim at the base lake when we get back and then use the hot tub."

Running her arm over her forehead, Shelly wiped some beads of sweat from her skin. "I'd love that." She didn't want to admit that her leg was aching and the idea of swimming and using a hot tub sounded like a great way to alleviate some of the discomfort in her limb.

When Shelly indicated she was ready to go on, the girls moved up the winding path through the forest with the scent of pine trees floating on the light breeze and the babbling rush of river water like music in the air. The effort of climbing the hill amidst the natural beauty filled Shelly with exhilaration and it had been a long time since she'd felt so good. Reaching the flat part of the trail, the young women had room to walk side by side.

"We're coming up to the crooked trees," Juliet said. "They start just around the bend."

She didn't know why, but a flutter of unease ran through Shelly's chest. Although the oddly-shaped trees interested her, every time Juliet mentioned them she felt anxious.

When they rounded the bend in the trail, Shelly came to a halt. A path meandered through a grove of pine trees that were bent and twisted just as Juliet had described. All of the trees' trunks on the left side bent slightly to the right pointing in the direction of the path and the trees on the right side, bent a little to the left giving an impression that the pines were like arms gesturing the visitor forward. Light filtered down between the branches giving the space a golden glow. Many of the trees seemed to be the same distance apart as if someone had deliberately planted them in the unusual arrangement. Shelly expected to see about twenty trees in the crooked collection, but the odd pines stretched out before her like a hundred sentries guarding the section of forest by keeping a traveler to the path.

"What do you think?" Juliet asked.

"I think it's one of the weirdest things I've ever seen. Maybe *the* weirdest." Shelly stepped closer to one of the trees to get a better look at the bent trunk and she ran her hand over the bark. "Did someone plant these and bend the trunks?"

"No one knows for sure." Juliet followed Shelly as she walked between the pines. "It would take an awful lot of work to manage the bending of all these trees."

"What do you think caused it?"

"I've read about them and the different ideas given by townspeople, plant biologists, anthropologists. No one has come up with a definitive theory. I really have no idea." Juliet walked around one of the larger pines. "It's good we came so early. I think it takes away from the first sight of the trees when the tourists are buzzing around."

"I agree." Shelly stood still and then turned in a circle gazing at the odd configuration. "It's equal parts weird, eerie, and cool." Giving Juliet a look, she said, "I'm still going with the suggestion that aliens did it."

Juliet chuckled. "Like Stonehenge, Machu Picchu, and the statues on Easter Island."

Shelly kidded, "I didn't know aliens were responsible for those things, too."

"Some people will believe any crazy idea." Juliet walked along the path. "Want to go a little further? There's a small lake up ahead with fields of wildflowers around it. It's really pretty."

Shelly agreed and the two set off making their way between the crooked trees until the area opened up and the trail curved past two meadows and all the while they walked, she couldn't push thoughts of the woman's murder from her mind. "Where was Meg Stores's body found? You mentioned she was discovered not far from the crooked trees."

"There's a narrow path up ahead that veers off to the right. She was found down that way by some hikers."

"That had to be an awful discovery." Not wanting to appear ghoulish, Shelly didn't ask if the body was found in a pond like she'd seen in her dream. Letting out a breath of relief, she was certain she must have read or heard about the murder and that her dream must have pulled at the pieces of information that had been stored in her brain.

The crystal, blue lake spread out before them and the branches of weeping willow trees hung gracefully over the edges of the water. Wildflowers bloomed in the fields around the perfect body of water and there was a sweet scent of berries or flowers on the air. The girls followed a tiny path around the lake and then headed back towards the crooked forest.

"I haven't walked this much for a long time."

Juliet gave Shelly a look of concern. "I shouldn't have dragged you so far."

"I'll be sore tomorrow, but I wouldn't have missed it," Shelly said. "It's been a great morning ... and I'm looking forward to that soak in the hot tub."

Shelly swung her backpack from her shoulder, unzipped it, and reached for her water bottle. The cylinder slipped through her hand, hit the ground, and rolled down the hill with the young woman chasing after it. The bottle veered to the right and came to rest in some underbrush beneath a tall oak tree. Shelly bent to pick it up and her hand froze in mid-air as something at the corner of her peripheral vision caught her attention. Kneeling on one leg, she blinked at a spot about thirty yards away as Juliet came up beside her.

Something red stuck out from under the long branches of the thick bushes and Shelly narrowed her eyes trying to make out what it was.

It looked like a red athletic shoe.

Juliet followed her new friend's gaze. "What's that over there?"

As the young woman headed to see, a rush of worry flooded Shelly's body and she said to her companion, "Wait a second. Maybe you shouldn't...."

Shelly stood up and approached just as Juliet poked her toe at the red thing. In less than a half-second, a high-pitched, ear-splitting noise like a siren pierced the air.

It was the sound of Juliet's scream.

4

———

It was late afternoon before Shelly put the key in the lock of the cottage door, went inside, and sank onto the sofa, shell-shocked and exhausted. Luckily, there had been cell phone service on the mountain hiking trail so their emergency call could be placed to the police.

Juliet's scream caused Shelly to scurry back so quickly that she lost her balance and fell onto her backside where she ended up staring through the thin branches of the bushes to see a body on the ground under the shrubs. When Juliet had poked the red shoe with her toe, she saw it was attached to a leg, and her eyes, peeking between the leaves, traveled up from the limb to the person's form lying in the dirt beneath the underbrush.

It was so unexpected and so unreal that it took

Juliet's mind a couple of seconds to process the scene and when it did, it triggered a loud, piercing shriek that nearly froze Shelly's blood.

Jumping to her feet, Shelly had grabbed Juliet's arm and the two huddled together for a few minutes horrified by the discovery until one of them ... neither could remember who suggested it ... made the call to the police.

It seemed an eternity before law enforcement and the emergency medical personnel arrived. Shelly and Juliet had moved a hundred yards down the trail away from the body to sit on a fallen log and wait. Even though neither one's gaze had lingered on the dead body, they both knew it was a young woman.

"Did you recognize her?" Shelly had whispered.

Juliet shook her head, and then they remained quiet and pensive during the endless minutes until help finally showed up.

Officers questioned them over and over. The body was briefly examined by the paramedics. The medical examiner arrived. Investigators combed the area searching for clues. Juliet's sister, Jay, arrived and the two hugged for a long time. Juliet let some tears escape from her eyes as she told her sister how they'd found the young woman under the bushes.

Pushing a loose strand of hair from her eyes, Juliet remembered that Jay and Shelly had never met and she hastily introduced them. "I can't even think straight," she apologized.

Shelly understood the feeling. It was as if she was walking through a dream – a nightmare, really, where everything seemed foggy and unclear. Sounds seemed muffled, her vision swam, and she felt like she was watching the goings-on from outside of her body.

Jay, short for Jayne, in her early forties with chin-length brown hair, was tall, stocky, and strong-looking – her build the opposite of Juliet's – and was a twenty-year veteran of the police force. She escorted them down the trail to her waiting police department SUV and took them to the station to speak with a detective. After two more hours, they were free to go. Shelly's body felt charged and wired, but when she slumped down and rested her head back against the plump couch cushions, her eyes closed and she fell into a deep sleep.

A soft, incessant cry roused her from her dreamless nap and she stirred trying to determine where the noise was coming from. Sitting up straight, she rubbed her eyes and turned her head from side to side. Shadows filled the room and glancing to the window, she noticed it was getting dark outside. *I must have slept for hours.*

A mewing sound floated through the living room window screen causing Shelly to get up and open the front door. There on the porch sat a small calico cat. It looked up at Shelly and mewed.

Shelly was about to step onto the porch, but the kitty scooted inside, stood on its hind legs, stretched its paws up, and placed them on the young woman's leg. *Mew.*

Chuckling, Shelly bent to scratch the cat's cheeks admiring the white, orange, and black color pattern swirled in the fur. "Where did you come from, sweet girl?" Shelly knew that a calico cat was rarely a male.

The cat's purring filled the air as it rubbed its head against Shelly's hand.

"What's this? A visitor?" Juliet came up the porch steps to the open front door.

Shelly looked up with a smile. "She was mewing at the door. Do you recognize her from the neighborhood?"

"I've never seen her before." It was Juliet's turn to scratch the friendly animal's cheeks. "She's so distinctive, I would have noticed her roaming around."

They both sat on the wood floor allowing the cat

to move between them, rubbing her head against the two women and purring.

Juliet said, "Did you know that in some cultures, calico cats are thought to bring good luck?"

"I didn't know that." Shelly made eye contact with her neighbor. "Maybe it's a good thing she showed up."

"Jay came by." Juliet's face looked tense. "They've identified the body. There was a driver's license in the back pocket of her shorts."

"Was she from town?"

Juliet shook her head. "Her name is Jill Murray, twenty-nine. She came to interview for a teaching job and had been in town for about a week, scouting out the area, trying to decide if she wanted to move here if she was offered the job. She loved the outdoors."

"So...." The cat had settled in Shelly's lap and she moved her hand over its soft fur. "Two women, not from the area, one a recent move-in and the other one considering a move to Paxton Park." Shelly raised an eyebrow. "Someone doesn't like newcomers?"

"There are lots of people who are new to town. New ski instructors arrive each winter and then leave in the spring. Waitstaff changes all the time.

New employees arrive in summer to run the attractions, act as guides. Graduate students and professors come in all seasons to do different kinds of research. People come and go all the time in a resort area."

"I'm a newcomer." The corners of Shelly's mouth turned down. "And I'm similar in age and appearance to the two women who have been murdered. Not exactly a *welcome to the mountain*."

Juliet looked down at the cat. "I think everyone needs to be on guard, newcomer or not. Especially young women. Make sure you lock your door. Jay suggests we carry pepper spray."

Letting out a sigh, Shelly said, "A return to Boston is looking pretty good right now."

"Don't leave." Juliet looked sad. "It's nice having you here."

"I won't make any decisions yet." Still perched on Shelly's lap, the cat purred loudly as it closed its eyes. "What should I do about this newcomer?"

"Keep it." Juliet smiled.

"I think I'll call the local animal hospital and ask if she might be a patient. They might be able to figure out who the owner is."

"Good idea, but I get the feeling you just adopted

a cat. Or should I say, a cat has adopted you." Juliet tilted her head. "She'll need a name."

"Hmm." Shelly let out a sigh, the image of the red athletic shoe in her mind. "How about *Justice*?"

"Yes," Juliet said softly. "I think that's a good choice. Maybe this new cat will bring us all some good luck."

A frown pulled at Shelly's lips. "I think we're going to need it."

The young women decided to make tea and have something to eat so they sliced two pieces from the apple pie Juliet had made and delivered to Shelly the day before. They took their drinks and plates out to the porch table. Justice followed along, jumped up on the railing, and sat watching the road and listening to the night sounds of crickets and peepers, chirping and clicking.

"I know it's early in the investigation, but are there any indications that the two dead women might have had a connection?" Shelly lifted a bite of pie to her mouth.

"Jay said they don't know yet. Right now, they're trying to reach her next of kin."

"Where was she staying?"

"At the resort hotel. She was due to check out in a couple of days."

"She came alone?" Shelly asked.

"I don't think they know for sure yet."

"Do you know where she lived?"

"A town in central Massachusetts. Ashbury."

"I don't know it." Shelly shook her head.

The cat let out a soft mew, turned her head to the women sitting at the metal table, and then looked back to the sidewalk. A woman was hurrying along the sidewalk carrying a paper bag. She looked straight ahead and slightly downward as if she had no desire to engage in any pleasantries or conversation should she run into someone as she made her way along the lane.

"It's Maria Stores," Juliet whispered. "The sister of the first murdered woman."

Shelly watched as Maria hurried away and a thought popped into her mind. "Where was Meg Stores from?"

"I don't recall." Juliet took out her phone and tapped at the screen to do a search on Meg. When the information loaded, she read through the articles. "Here it is. She lived in Eastborough, Massachusetts."

"Where's that?" Shelly asked. "I don't know that town either."

Juliet tapped again and slid her phone across the

table so that Shelly could see. "Here's a map of the state. The little red flag on the map is where Eastborough is."

"Central Massachusetts." Shelly looked up, her forehead lined with concern. "Eastborough is only five miles from Ashbury."

"That's a coincidence, isn't it?"

"Could those women have known each other? Could they have had a mutual acquaintance?" Shelly's eyes were wide. "Could central Massachusetts be a link?"

"The police will look into it." Juliet tried to be reassuring. "Whatever it is, they'll figure it out."

"In the meantime," Shelly said with a determined tone, "I'm going to get myself some pepper spray."

Justice mewed her agreement from the porch railing.

A fter Juliet left, Shelly took some leftover chicken from the refrigerator and cut it into small pieces for the cat who eagerly gobbled it up. Looking up at the wall clock, she said out loud, "The market and the hardware store are still open. I'm going to go and get you some cat food and a litter box." Shelly stared at the new arrival. "Or are you an outside cat?"

Justice kept licking her paw and moving it over her face to groom herself.

"I'll be back." Shelly grabbed her keys and wallet and headed to the center of town. Entering the market, she found the aisle with cat food and chose several containers to put in her cart in addition to several toy mice she thought the calico might enjoy. Shelly was happy to see that the store carried plastic bins and kitty litter and she put those items in her shopping cart and headed for the checkout counter.

A couple of customers stood chatting with the owner.

"I can't believe it," one gray-haired woman fretted. "Nothing like this has ever happened in Paxton Park as long as I've lived here."

"A second murdered woman." A tall man shook his head. "The police better get on this fast or tourists will steer clear."

The owner leaned against the checkout counter shaking his head. He was medium-build, about five foot ten and had dark hair with gray streaks at his temples. His skin was tanned and kind of leathery from years of outdoor activities. "First Meg was found strangled, now someone else has been killed. It's been over two months since Meg died and there hasn't been an arrest. It's not a good sign."

Shelly approached the group and nodded. She was familiar to the owner as she'd done quite a bit of shopping in his store since moving to town.

"You heard the news?" the owner asked her. His name tag had the word *Chet* engraved in black letters.

"I did." Shelly didn't know if she should share that she was one of the people who had found the body, but then thought it would seem odd if Chet found out later that she and Juliet discovered Jill Murray in the woods and she'd said nothing. She gave the small group a brief description of what had happened near the crooked forest.

"Something evil must be in those woods." The older woman clutched her arms over her chest. "Two bodies in that area. Those trees. Maybe they harbor evil spirits."

"It's definitely something evil," Chet said, "but it's most likely a human being."

"It's all too much for me." The older woman gathered her grocery bags and left the store with the tall man.

"I'm sorry about your employee," Shelly said as Chet rang up her things. "I didn't know anything about it until recently."

"It was a shock, I'll tell you that. The whole town was abuzz when it happened, then it went on the back burner when no one was charged with the murder. People stopped talking about it. Now a second murder."

"What was Meg like?" Shelly asked gently.

Chet looked surprised at the question, but he answered. "She was a nice person, quiet, did her work."

"Did she have family?"

"An older sister. She's here in town for a few days. She came back to clean out the house her sister rented. I guess she couldn't face doing it at the time."

"I can understand that." Shelly thought of her own sister and about cleaning out Lauren's apartment after the car accident. When her throat tightened with emotion, she swallowed hard. "Did Meg seem happy here in town?"

Chet blinked a few times pondering. "I guess so. She didn't seem *un*happy. Like I said, she was quiet, a hard worker."

"Had she made some friends?"

Chet's shoulder went up. "Not sure. I didn't see her around much if she wasn't here at the market." The man paused. "Though I did see her at the candy store a few times talking to the blond girl who works there."

Shelly's interest piqued. "Do you know her name?"

"Um, I can't think of it." Chet put the cat food and toys into a bag. "You want the litter and the bin in a bag?"

Shelly shook her head. "Did Meg have anyone visit from home while she was here?"

"I don't think so. Meg never said anything about that."

"Did she ever say why she moved to Paxton Park?"

Chet took Shelly's cash and returned a few coins. "Meg said she needed a change. She liked nature and this place fit the bill." The man stroked his chin. "One time, she said something about feeling safe here. Ironic, huh?"

A shiver ran across Shelly's skin. "Did she talk about where she came from?"

"Not much. Her sister lived in New York. Meg wanted to do a lot skiing when winter came. She said her previous town was boring and she had to drive everywhere. She liked all the tourists here, the hustle and bustle. Meg liked that she could walk to all the stores and restaurants in Paxton Park and didn't have to use a car."

Shelly liked that about the town, too. If she could avoid it, she'd never get back in a car again and was perfectly happy to use her feet or her bicycle to get around.

"What did Meg do for work before she came here? Did she work in a market?"

"Meg was a real estate agent. She was working part-time at Park Realty, helping out the listing

43

agent. She told me she wasn't sure if she wanted to continue in real estate, but she wanted to make contacts just in case."

"I wonder why she didn't want to work as an agent anymore."

"I asked, but she didn't say much." Chet put the bag of cat items and the small bag of litter inside the plastic box. "This way it will be easier to carry home."

"Thanks." Shelly picked up her things and headed for the door wishing Chet a goodnight.

"Be careful out there." Chet made eye contact with the young woman. "Keep on your toes."

Shelly stepped out into the darkness and even though the sidewalks were lit by streetlamps, the night suddenly felt oppressive and made her painfully aware that she was alone. Holding tightly to the cat box, she walked faster, her heart pounding. Every few seconds, she thought she heard footsteps coming up behind and she took quick glances over her shoulder to see. The awkwardness of carrying the box kept her from bolting down the streets and she berated herself for not waiting until morning to run the errand. Keeping up a brisk pace, Shelly turned down her road thankful that she was almost home.

Passing by Juliet's cottage, she let out a sigh of relief and was ashamed for letting the talk of the murdered women spook her so badly. A few houses down on the other side of the street, a figure burst through the front door of the bungalow and tore down the porch steps, ran across the street, and headed towards Shelly.

Shelly stopped in her tracks, startled by the sudden movement of the person. A flash of anxiety ran through her body. Should she stay on the sidewalk? Should she run for her house? Should she turn and run into Juliet's cottage? Even though the options zipped in her mind in a matter of milliseconds, the dark figure nearly bashed into her on its mad dash along the dark sidewalk.

Adrenaline coursing through her veins, Shelly let the items she was holding drop to the ground and she lifted her arms up in a defensive posture.

The person gasped, halted, and when she saw Shelly, reached out and took her arm. "Can you help me?" It was Maria, the sister of Meg Stores.

For a split second, Shelly thought her request for help was a trick of some sort, but getting a look at the woman's face pushed her suspicions away. "What is it? What's wrong?"

Maria clutched hard to Shelly's arm and took a

glance back to the house her sister had been renting. "In the house. I heard something at the back door, like someone was trying to break in."

"Why don't you come inside with me?" Shelly gestured to her cottage. "We can call the police."

Maria's expression was tentative, but then she nodded. As Shelly picked up the things she'd dropped, Maria apologized. "I startled you. I'm so sorry. I didn't see you in the dark. I just wanted to get away."

Shelly gave the woman a reassuring smile. "It's okay. Come in with me."

When the door swung open, the calico cat was waiting, sitting calmly just inside, its long tail swung around its front paws.

Shelly removed her phone from the pocket in her wallet and handed it to Maria. "You can use my phone to call the police."

Maria held the phone, but when she didn't make a move to place the emergency call, Shelly asked, "Don't you want to call them?"

"What if I was hearing things?"

"It's okay," Shelly encouraged. "They can take a look. It will make you feel better if they go through the house."

Maria gave a slight nod, made the call, and then said to Shelly, "I'm sorry to bother you."

"It's no bother." Shelly offered a drink, but Maria declined.

"Have a seat while we wait."

When the cat jumped up to sit beside the shaken woman and Maria stroked the multi-colored fur, Shelly noticed a crumpled piece of paper in the woman's other hand. "The cat showed up on my doorstep today. Have you seen her around the neighborhood?"

"I haven't. She's lovely. I would have noticed a cat like this."

Maria's tension seemed to slip away slightly as she patted the small, friendly animal so Shelly asked her about what she'd heard in the house.

"I was going through Meg's papers. I started to get upset. There was a noise at the backdoor in the kitchen, a scratching, a sound like something metal scratching at the doorknob. I panicked, afraid Meg's killer had come to the house." Maria shook her head slowly. "I probably imagined it."

"It's possible that someone knew the house was empty and decided to break in. You did the right thing to get out of there. Let the police take a look." Shelly

47

realized that she hadn't offered condolences to the distraught woman so she told Maria how sorry she was for the loss of her sister. Although Shelly wanted to ask some questions about Meg, she knew it wasn't the right time to do it so she stayed quiet. "Shall we go out to the porch so we can see when the police arrive?"

Maria stilled clutched the piece of paper in her hand. Looking up, she seemed to be struggling with something. At last, she passed the paper to Shelly and said, "I found this in Meg's things."

Shelly smoothed out the paper and when she read the words written in black ink, a shot of fear pulsed in her veins.

I'm going to get you

6

The police arrived, walked through the dead woman's house, and checked the lock on the back door. "It looks like someone *was* picking at the lock," the officer said.

Maria went pale.

"It wasn't a professional. It was probably some kid or some young guy who thought it might be entertaining to break in and look around."

Maria sank into a chair at the kitchen table.

"You have the lights on a timer?" the officer asked.

"Yes." Maria's voice was barely audible.

"You're staying at the resort, right? Not here at the house?"

"That's right. I don't want to stay here." Maria bit her lower lip.

"The guy most likely came by on a few nights, saw the lights on, figured they must be on a timer, and came back tonight to break in." The officer shook his head. "It wouldn't take a lot of skill to pick this lock. Whoever it was doesn't know what he's doing. It's doubtful the attempt had anything to do with the person who was responsible for your sister's death."

Shelly stood near the counter and glanced over to Maria. The police officer's information wasn't that comforting. Any person would be filled with fear no matter who tried to break into a house, but ... it *was* reassuring that the *killer* wasn't attempting to terrorize his victim's relative.

Before the officers left the bungalow, Maria showed them the piece of paper she'd found in her sister's files. A look of surprise passed over their faces and the senior officer put on gloves to handle the sheet and slip it into an evidence bag. "Did you come across anything else like this?"

Maria gave a slight shake of her head. Shelly thought the woman looked like she was about to pass out and brought a glass of water over to her.

"We'll deliver this to the detective in charge." The officers assured Maria that the note would get the attention it deserved, told her to keep the doors locked, and then Shelly walked them to the door.

Returning to the kitchen, she sat in the chair across from Maria who looked weak and exhausted. "Can I get you anything?" Shelly asked. "Tea? A glass of wine?"

"No, thank you. There isn't anything here anyway."

"Would you like to come back to my place?"

Maria tried to smile, but without success. "No. I don't want to take any more of your time. You've been very kind to me."

Shelly got the feeling that the woman wanted to talk so she waited quietly to see if Maria would start a conversation. When she didn't initiate, Shelly said softly, "I lost my sister not long ago, my twin sister."

Maria raised her eyes.

"We were on the highway. Lauren was driving. Her boyfriend was in the back seat. There was a bang. It was something called a tie rod, it had to do with the steering gear. There was no way to steer the car." Shelly took in a deep breath. "We smashed into a cement barrier and the car flew into the air. I don't remember anything after that, but the police told me the car flipped over several times. Lauren and her boyfriend were killed. I was in the hospital for a long time." Shelly brushed at her eyes. "Lauren was more than a sister to me, she was my best friend."

"I'm very sorry," Maria whispered. A tear rolled down her cheek and she cleared her throat. "Meg and I weren't close. I'm fifteen years older than she was. We were always at different points in life. I've been so busy with my career. I live in New York. I never made time for her." Maria's voice broke. "If I paid more attention to Meg...." Her voice trailed off.

"It's not your fault." Shelly's voice was gentle.

"Maybe it is. Maybe if I'd shown more interest, she wouldn't have moved here and...."

Shelly held Maria's eyes. "And if my sister and I weren't on that highway, Lauren would still be alive. It doesn't do any good to speculate or to torture ourselves with *what ifs*."

"I feel like I wasted an opportunity," Maria said. "At least you and your sister were close. I've lost the chance to know my sister, to have a relationship with her. It's gone. It slipped through my fingers. I can never get it back."

Shelly didn't know which was worse, losing someone you were close to and loved, or having the chance to build a relationship with someone ripped from your hands. In the end, it didn't matter. Loss was loss, and it tore a hole right through your heart.

"Had you talked to Meg before she died?" Shelly asked.

"We talked on the phone the week before it happened."

"How did she sound? Was she worried about anything?"

Maria gave a shrug. "If she was, she probably wouldn't have confided in me. We didn't share things like that. It was always just superficial chat."

"So you didn't pick up on anything in her tone or in what she said?"

"No."

"Where did you find the note?"

"In Meg's files. It was in a folder with a bunch of bills."

"Was there an envelope with it?" Shelly hoped there was an envelope since it would give information about where and when the letter was mailed.

"No."

"Then it could have been in there for some time. It could even have been written by your sister."

Maria's eyebrows shot up. "Why would she do that?"

"I don't know, but it's a possibility." Shelly thought of something else. "The police must have gone through your sister's things after she died. They must have missed seeing that note."

"It was stuffed in with all the bills. They would have had to go through the papers one by one. They mustn't have done that."

Shelly asked, "Did your sister know anyone who lived here in town? Is that one of the reasons she moved here?"

"I don't know."

"Did Meg know the other woman who was found in the woods? Jill Murray?"

Something seemed to pass over Maria's face, but it was gone in a flash. "I don't know." Rubbing her forehead, she said, "I think I'll go back to the hotel now. I'm so tired."

"Do you have a car?"

"I'll call a cab." Maria stood up and glanced at a milk crate full of files. "Would you mind taking this crate to your house? It's full of the last six months of Meg's real estate files from Eastborough and I don't know if it's necessary to keep them. I can pick them up from you another day. I don't want to lug them in the cab with me."

"Sure, I'd be glad to." Shelly picked up the container.

"Thank you for your help," Maria said. "I can't thank you enough."

"Come by anytime." Shelly gave a smile. "You know where I live."

She left the bungalow and walked to her house. The calico was waiting at the door when she opened it. Shelly gave the cat a pat and then stepped back. "Do you want to go out? Do you want to go back to your home?"

The cat turned around and headed for Shelly's bedroom where she leapt up onto the bed, settled, and began to press her front paws alternately against the pillow. Her purrs filled the air.

"I'll take that as a no." Shelly chuckled, put the crate by the bookcase in her room, got ready for bed, and crawled under the covers with her new pet leaning against her back. The deep rhythmic purring relaxed the young woman and in a matter of minutes, she drifted off to sleep.

～

JUSTICE MEWED RIGHT next to the young woman's face. Half-asleep, Shelly opened one eye. "It's too early. Go back to sleep, kitty."

Rolling onto her other side, Shelly sensed lights

moving across the wall of her bedroom and both of her eyes flew open. Blue lights pulsed rhythmically from the window, but there was another, different type of light coming from outside – reddish, flickering. The scent of something floated in through the window screen.

Justice let out a howl and Shelly sat up to attention.

Fire.

Dashing out of bed, she peered outside. Flames shot through the roof of one of the houses on the street. Shelly slipped into shoes and ran for the front door, her heart pounding. When she stepped onto the porch, Juliet ran up the steps.

"I was going to wake you," Juliet was breathless. She pointed. "The house. It's on fire."

Its siren screaming, a fire truck roared around the corner from Main Street and tore down the road.

Shelly leaned over the porch railing to see better and her heart dropped. "Meg Stores's house?"

Juliet nodded and stood next to Shelly, her eyes trained on the roaring, crackling fire. Sitting on the rail, Justice flicked her tail back and forth as she watched the flames against the inky sky. The red-orange inferno cast an eerie glow over the neighborhood and the smell of burning materials made Shelly's nostrils sting.

"I was just in that house several hours ago."

Juliet turned with her mouth open. "Why?"

For the next few minutes, Shelly gave an account of her evening from the time Juliet left her to when she awoke just now to the sight of the blaze.

"Maria said she was going back to the hotel. She said she'd call a cab." Shelly's face clouded. "Did she leave the house or did she stay there? Is she inside? Did someone set the fire with her in there?"

"Maybe another question might be ... did she set it herself?" Juliet asked.

Shelly moved her hand to the side of her face. "I didn't think of that. But, why would *she* set the house on fire?"

Juliet looked back down the street. "Maybe there's something in there she doesn't want anyone to find."

"I wonder," Shelly said. "The police supposedly went through Meg's things. They could have overlooked something important. They overlooked the note."

"Or did they?" One of Juliet's eyebrows went up.

Nervousness zipped through Shelly's body. "Do you think Maria could have written that note herself? Do you think she made up the story of finding it in the files?"

"Things get more complicated by the day, don't they," Juliet noted with a frown.

For the next hour, the two women and the cat watched the firefighters battle the blaze.

What next? Shelly wondered with a nervous shiver. *What next?*

7

Unable to return to sleep, Shelly arrived at the diner early to start the day's baking. She and Juliet made plans to meet for dinner with hopes of sharing some news they might discover from talking to people about the fire at Meg Stores's rented house.

Before going to the diner, Shelly stopped at the resort hotel to inquire about Maria Stores and the desk clerk informed her that Ms. Stores had checked out late last night, after midnight. Although surprised by the news, Shelly was relieved that Maria was not a victim of the fire, but nagging questions about the woman swirled in her head and she could not push away the idea that Maria might have fabricated the story about the note. Shelly hoped that Juliet would learn some details about the fire and the note from her sister, Jay.

"Well, look what the cat dragged in," Henry called when Shelly entered the diner.

Henry's wife, Melody, a short, silver-haired woman in her sixties with bright blue eyes, was setting up the coffee maker and her expression was filled with concern. "We heard about the fire. You must have been awake half the night."

"I was." Shelly pulled an apron over her head. "It was an awful sight to see that house on fire. It didn't seem real."

"Henry and I have been talking about it since we got up." Melody filled the sugar containers and placed them on the tables. "We think it has to be connected to that poor woman's murder. But, why would the killer set her house on fire?"

Shelly had been thinking the same thing, but also wondered, if it was the killer who set the fire, why wait to do it? Why not burn it down right after committing the crime?

Henry carried cartons of eggs to set next to the kitchen grill. "It may not be arson at all. It could be a faulty electrical system that caused the fire to start. We can't jump to conclusions. Anyway, I heard the sister of the murdered girl was here cleaning out the house. Maybe she left a stove burner on or maybe she put a cigarette in the trash."

Shelly told the couple about running into Maria last night, the call to the police because of the suspected break-in attempt, and the note Maria claimed to have found in her sister's files.

Melody and Henry stared at Shelly.

"Good grief," Melody said softly, her face screwed up with worry. "The killer really came to the house?"

"The police thought it might be kids trying to break in for a lark." Shelly took flour and sugar from the cabinet.

"Then the house gets set on fire?" Henry shook his head as he flipped over some hash browns on the grill. "That wasn't kids that did it. No way."

"What do you think is going on?" Shelly asked.

"I'm not a cop. I have no idea." Henry salted the hash browns spread over the grill. "But now I bet its more than just a house fire. It has to have some connection to the murder."

"Maybe something was in the house that someone didn't want discovered." Shelly looked up to see Melody and Henry looking at her with troubled expressions.

"Why can't this be solved?" Melody asked. "It's

going on too long, more terrible things have happened. Where will it end?"

"The police will figure it out." Henry tried to be comforting, but Shelly could see deep worry lines pressed into the man's forehead.

"Did you know Meg Stores?" she asked.

Melody wiped her hands on a dish towel. "She used to come in for breakfast a few times a week. We'd chat. Henry would banter with her."

Henry seemed to wince at the memory of the young woman.

"Did Meg seem worried or upset before she went missing?"

Melody said, "We didn't notice at the time, but when we looked back on it, we thought she'd been quieter than usual."

"Did she ever talk about the town she moved away from?" Shelly took some butter from the refrigerator. "Did she ever mention anything that was bothering her like breaking up with a boyfriend or having a run-in with someone?"

"I don't recall anything like that." Melody put the cash drawer into the register. "We didn't get into anything deep. It was only friendly chit chat." The woman stopped what she was doing and looked off out of the window. "I can't believe what's happened. I can't believe that poor girl was killed."

"What about Meg's sister, Maria? Did she ever come into the diner while she was here?"

"A few times." Melody made a face. "She was the opposite of Meg. There was something hard or distant about her. She had no interest in conversation. She had no interest in interaction at all. The woman was downright rude."

"The woman had suffered a loss." Henry spoke through the serving window. "She was probably afraid that conversing would lead to questions about her sister."

As Shelly was returning to the back room, she said, "Maria checked out of the resort after midnight last night."

"Hmm." Henry's eyes narrowed in suspicion. "What was her rush? Leaving so late? Why not wait until the next morning?"

"Good question." Shelly mixed the softened butter into the batter.

Melody came into the back room and forced a chuckle, but her eyes looked tired and worried. "Did the sister set the fire and then take off?"

"I've been wondering that very thing," Shelly said with a serious face.

Melody's eyes widened at Shelly's comment, but then turned quickly to check the wall clock like she needed a distraction from the speculation. "Almost time to open." She let out a sigh. "Now I look at everyone who comes into the diner with suspicion. Are you the killer? Am I serving a murderer? That's what I think. I don't like being distrustful of people, but I just can't help it." On her way out of the work room to unlock the front door for the customers, Melody said, "I have to push it all from mind. I can't allow myself to dwell on it."

Shelly didn't seem to be able to do that. The images of finding Jill Murray's dead body on the mountainside kept flashing in her mind. Her interaction with Maria Stores played over and over in her head. The hiss and roar of the fire tearing away at the neighborhood house echoed in her ears.

To distract herself from the mysteries, Shelly threw herself into the baking, visited the bakery manager on the other side of the kitchen to discuss what they would need over the next few days, and carried platters of fresh sweets to the glass cases in the diner.

The morning passed quickly and it was nearly 2pm when the day's baking tasks had been completed ... which happened to coincide with the wave of fatigue that hit Shelly as she was putting the clean cookie sheets away. "I'm worn out. I need a nap."

Melody stuck her head into the work room. "Shelly? There's someone out here who wants to talk to you."

Anxiety rushed through Shelly's veins. "Who is it?"

"A detective," Melody said in a hushed tone. "He said his name is Andrew Walton."

Hesitating for a moment, Shelly took a deep breath and stepped forward. "Okay." There were only a few people in the diner when she walked out of the back room to meet the detective and she spotted him right away. Sitting at a table in the corner, he was tall and slim with dark blond hair, about thirty years old, and wore chinos, a pale blue buttoned-down shirt, and a dark blue tie. He stood up when Shelly approached.

"I'm Shelly Taylor." She shook hands with the man and sat down.

"Andrew Walton. Thanks for talking with me."

Feeling unsettled and nervous, Shelly swallowed to clear her throat and folded her hands in her lap.

"I'd like to ask some questions about last night."

"Okay."

"Could you give me a rundown of your evening?"

Giving a nod, Shelly provided a detailed account of what she'd done the previous afternoon and night starting with her arrival home from finding the body in the woods to waking up to the house fire. "It was an eventful eighteen hours."

Detective Walton kept an expressionless face. "Where did you live before coming to Paxton Park?"

Shelly thought the detective must know quite a bit about her since she'd spent two hours the previous day at the police station with another detective going over what had happened in the woods and how she and Juliet had come upon the body. "Boston."

"What made you leave the city?"

Shelly stiffened. "I needed a change."

"I understand you and your sister were in a car accident."

"And Lauren's boyfriend ... yes."

The detective offered his condolences and then made eye contact with Shelly. "You've been involved in several unusual circumstances recently."

Shelly tilted her head in question.

"The fatal car accident, discovering the body of Ms. Murray yesterday, and the fire last night."

Her cheeks flushed red as a surge of anger filled

Shelly's chest. Was the detective insinuating that she'd had something to do with the three events? "What is that supposed to mean?" She forced her tone to remain even.

"I'm just pointing out that you've been involved in some unfortunate happenings, that's all."

"I'm fully aware of what I've had to deal with." Shelly sat up straight keeping her eyes locked on the detective. "I don't need any reminders."

"I apologize. What time did you leave Maria Stores last night?"

"It was around 11:30, maybe closer to midnight."

"She checked out of the hotel shortly after that."

Shelly waited.

"We haven't been able to locate Ms. Stores."

"You called her at home?" Shelly asked. "Her cell number?"

"We did. Do you happen to have a contact number for her? Maybe she has multiple phones."

"We exchanged cell numbers." Shelly got up to get her phone and returned to the detective's table. "Here it is." She read the numbers from her contact list.

The detective thanked her. "We've been in contact with the police in New York. They went to her apartment, but no one was at home."

"Maybe she's staying with a friend."

"You haven't heard from her?" the detective asked.

Shelly's eyes widened. "No."

"Did she tell you where she might be headed?"

"No." Shelly shook her head. "I didn't even know Maria was leaving town. She didn't say a word about it. I thought she'd be staying here for a while longer since she still had things to clear out of the house."

"Well, thanks for your time." The detective reached across the table to shake hands. "I'm sure Ms. Stores will show up." He smiled, nodded, and left the diner.

Shelly's throat tightened. *Ms. Stores will show up? Are they worried something has happened to Maria? What's going on?*

8

As Shelly put the tacos in the oven, Justice ran to the living room when she heard Juliet knock and enter the house. Carrying a big bowl of salad, Juliet greeted the cat and headed to the kitchen. "Smells great in here."

"It's beef and vegetable tacos. They'll be ready in a few minutes. I made a coconut cake for dessert."

"I think I just died and went to Heaven." Juliet gazed at the luscious three-layer cake and licked her lips.

"How's this kitty cat?" Juliet bent to scratch the cheeks of the calico as it wound around her legs.

"I called the town vet and she had no recollection of such an animal in her practice. I tried some of the neighboring animal rescue places to see if someone reported a missing cat, but Justice didn't match any descriptions."

"So it seems you have a new friend." The cat trilled at the words and Juliet smiled. "And she seems very happy about it."

Shelly placed napkins at the place settings. "I wasn't planning on having a pet, but I guess a small, calico feline had other ideas."

The kitchen table was set in front of sliding glass doors that looked out over the compact, grassy backyard. A tall Maple tree provided shade on hot summer days and flowering hydrangeas ringed the edge of the small property. The setting sun painted the sky with streaks of dark blue, pink, and violet.

Shelly removed the tacos from the oven, lit the candle on the table, and then they sat down to the tasty looking meal. A pleasant breeze entered through the open glass doors.

"A detective came to the diner to see me today." Shelly passed a bowl of Spanish rice to Juliet. "I didn't like some of the things he said to me."

"Who was it? What did he say?"

"Andrew Walton. Tall, slim, blond. He made remarks about how I'd been involved in some unusual circumstances."

Juliet lifted two tacos onto her plate. "He's right. You have."

"It made me feel like he thought I was responsible for the incidents."

Juliet looked across the table at her friend. "He was probably trying to unnerve you so you'd speak freely."

Shelly's jaw set. "It made me want to clam up."

"What else did he say?"

"He asked me to give an account of the day we found the body and the night I met Maria Stores. He said they haven't been able to get in touch with Maria." Shelly made eye contact with Juliet. "The way he said it made me think something has happened to her."

Juliet put down her glass of ice water, a look of concern on her face. "You think someone kidnapped her after you left the house?"

"I don't know. My stomach filled with anxiety when the detective said they couldn't find Maria. I can't get it out of my head that something bad has happened."

"Jay said the police have taken that note Maria claims she found in her sister's files and will have it analyzed for fingerprints. She said they don't have any solid leads in either murder case. Every angle is being investigated, but nothing has panned out yet."

"Not very encouraging." Shelly's heart sank. "They must think the deaths are linked?"

"They're going on that assumption, yeah."

"Are there surveillance cameras at the mountain?" Shelly asked.

"There are cameras around the resort area ... the hotel, diner, bakery, the other dining and coffee spots, but there isn't anything near the trails or the woods or the lake."

"The two women's bodies were found not far from one another," Shelly noted. "Is there any reason for someone to be in that location? Do guides take hikers or bike tours by the crooked trees? Are there any particular cross trails that pass there, like fire roads or something? Anything that would make escaping the area easy?"

"There's a fire road not far from where we found Jill Murray."

"Has Jay said anything about where the police think the women were killed? In the woods? At another location and then dropped in the woods?"

"Law enforcement's current theory is that the killer may have parked a vehicle on the fire road or maybe he hid a bike in some underbrush. The person waited for Jill to come by and then attacked as she looked at the crooked trees. They're still unsure if Meg was killed in the woods or in another location."

"I suppose that could mean the attacks were random." Shelly's mind raced.

"It could also have been planned. The killer didn't necessarily use a car or bike to escape. Jay disagrees with the idea. She thinks that using some kind of transportation would make the killer too conspicuous. Jay thinks the guy attacked the women and then hiked away. A hiker would be less obvious than someone driving away on the fire roads and the guy could keep to isolated trails on foot. He could have parked at any of the small parking spots around the mountain. There are lots of them."

"If it was planned, is the thought that the killer followed Meg and Jill into the woods and kept his distance until the moment he attacked?"

"That's what they think."

"The guy must have good skills in order to follow someone in the forest without being heard or seen. He must be an outdoorsman ... or maybe, ex-military?"

Juliet smiled. "That's exactly what Jay told me today. Nothing official has been said, but that's what she and a couple of the other officers have been talking about on their own. They think the killer is strong and has a good sense of the outdoors and is probably very familiar with the area trail system."

"When I went to the market last night, the owner, Chet, was talking to a couple of people about the murders. I joined them. Chet told me that Meg Stores had been a real estate agent before moving here. Meg wasn't sure she wanted to stay in the business, but she was working part time at Park Realty helping out in the office."

Juliet said, "Park Realty is the agency I used when I bought my house."

"Who was the agent you worked with?"

"The owner of the place. Lisa Bennett." Juliet leaned forward. "We should talk to her, ask about Meg. Maybe she could give us some information." Standing up, she crossed the kitchen to get her phone from the counter. "I've met up with her a few times for a drink. She's just a little older than us. I'll text her right now and ask if she can get together some time."

Shelly was hopeful that the woman would be willing to meet to talk about her ex-employee. Looking out at the darkening yard, she realized that something had been nagging at her ever since the fire, but she hadn't yet been able to sort out what it was.

"Lisa suggests we come out to meet her in an hour. She'll be at the pub at the resort."

Shelly nodded agreement and Juliet sent the reply.

"Meg and Jill must have something in common besides running into a crazy person." Shelly ate the last of her salad. "Or are you thinking the killer randomly chose them?"

Juliet thought for a few moments. "Don't ask me why, but I don't think it was random. I think he picked them for a reason."

"I have the same feeling. I don't think he was waiting in the woods for a victim. Maybe he didn't know them, but there was some reason why he chose those two women."

"They looked alike," Juliet said, and then added, "they also look like us. Our hair color isn't exactly the same, but we all have long hair, slim builds, athletic bodies. Sometimes, that worries me."

"Don't ever go into the woods alone." Shelly's voice was forceful. "We shouldn't walk alone anywhere that's isolated. We need to be on guard. Just in case."

"The murders have made me think twice about

where I'm going and how I'll get there. I always go for a run where I know people will be around." Juliet squared her shoulders. "I don't like having to change my life because of a nut."

"I know … I feel the same. If that's the way to stay safe, though, then that's what we have to do."

They cleared the table and Shelly set out dessert plates and cut the coconut cake.

Juliet practically swooned at the first bite. "This is fabulous. No wonder they hired you to be the baker." She licked the frosting from her fork. "If you weren't already employed, I'd have to hire you to be my personal baker."

Shelly chuckled. "Then you'd have to up your exercise regime. My repertoire is loaded with calories."

Juliet groaned. "Don't say another word. Let me enjoy this."

"Actually, it's not that bad. I've experimented with different ingredients and recipes to make my baked goods as tasty and as healthy as possible."

"I love you," Juliet kidded. "I'm so glad you live next door to me."

The conversation caused something to ping in Shelly's head, but trying to grasp what it was only caused the notion to float away from her.

"We haven't thought much about Jill Murray," Shelly said. "We've been focusing on Meg."

"That's because Meg lived here. Jill was only staying for a few days for her teaching interview. Nobody knew her."

Justice padded in from the living room and let out a high-pitched howl that caused both young women to jump.

"What's wrong, little one?" Shelly patted her lap to invite the calico to come sit with her. "No need to screech like that. You have a home now. You're not alone anymore."

As the cat leapt onto Shelly's lap, moved in a circle, and then settled down purring, some words kept repeating in Shelly's head.

Nobody knew her. Nobody knew her.

9

"**S**hall we walk to the resort?" Shelly asked Juliet as they descended from the porch on the way to meet the real estate broker to talk about Meg Stores.

"It's dark," Juliet had responded. "Let's take my car."

Ever since the accident, Shelly did everything she could to avoid riding in automobiles and the two-mile drive to the resort pub in Juliet's small car seemed like an eternity and caused her blood pressure to rise and sweat to trickle down her back. When the car pulled into a parking place, she practically leapt from the vehicle before the engine had even stopped.

They found Lisa Bennett, the owner of Park Realty, standing at the bar with a group of men and women who were chatting and laughing together. In her early thirties, Lisa was a tall, slim redhead with her hair cascading down her back in long ringlets. She was dressed in a short, black skirt, white blouse, and a pale yellow blazer. Spotting Juliet walking towards her in the crowded pub, Lisa waved her over.

The pub had a glossy wooden bar and huge windows that looked out towards the mountains. A country-rock band played in one corner of the place.

"Nice to meet you," Lisa beamed at Shelly with a wide, friendly smile as she moved with the young women to a newly-vacated table.

After ordering drinks and making some preliminary pleasantries, Juliet brought up Meg Stores. "Shelly lives next door to me. She was in Meg's house with Meg's sister, Maria, just a few hours before the fire started. We stood together watching the place burn." Juliet gave an involuntary shudder. "It shook us up."

"I rented that house to Meg." Lisa sipped from her wine glass. "That's how I met her." She turned to look out the window at the dark trees and the mountain. "I can't believe what happened."

"She worked for you?" Shelly asked.

Lisa shifted her attention away from the window.

"Part time. She helped out in the office, helped out the listing agent, answered calls. She was a pleasant person. She added a nice vibe to the team."

"How long had she worked for you?"

"Let's see. How long ago did she move to town? She started in the office right after we finalized the rental agreement for the house."

Juliet asked, "Meg had been a real estate agent before moving here?"

"She was. She told me she wasn't sure if she wanted to continue with the career. She liked real estate, but wanted something with regular hours. She didn't want to meet clients at all hours of the day and night."

"That was the reason she didn't want to work as an agent?" Shelly questioned. "She wanted more regular hours?"

Lisa sighed. "That was part of it."

"There was more to it than wanting regular hours?" Juliet leaned slightly forward.

"Meg had a bad experience."

A shot of adrenaline raced through Shelly's body.

"She was running an open house. A man came in to see the place. He pretended interest and called Meg to see the house again. He decided against making an offer, but asked to see a number of other homes that were on the market. Meg started to get a strange feeling from the guy, nothing overt, but she let him know she wouldn't be able to work with him anymore and handed him over to another agent."

"How did that go?" Shelly asked.

"The man kept contacting Meg ... calling, emailing. This guy even showed up outside Meg's home on a few occasions. He was a real pain. She told me she wasn't sure if the guy was interested in her romantically and this was his awkward way of showing attention or if he was a creep. She didn't want to take a chance. She had no interest in him. Finally, she told the guy that the real reason she had to let some clients go was that she had a health problem. The only problem Meg had was this guy bothering her."

"Did he accept her explanation?"

"At last, it seemed he did. He stopped contacting her." Lisa shook her head. "This can be a tough business. I'm often alone at open houses or when I'm showing a house to a client. It's very important to stay vigilant and not let your guard down."

"Did this happen in her home town?" Juliet asked.

Lisa gave a nod.

"Did Meg tell you when it happened?" Shelly asked. "Was it recent or some time ago?"

"She said it happened a year before she moved here."

"How about the guy's name? Did she mention it?"

"She might have, but I don't recall what it was."

"Did the police talk to you about Meg?" Juliet questioned.

"They did, yes." Lisa's happy mood had flattened from the topic of conversation. "I don't think I was any help."

"Did you tell them about this guy who bothered Meg?"

"I did. I bet they looked into it. I bet the agency that Meg used to work for would recall the incident. Maybe someone there remembers the guy's name."

Shelly exchanged a look with Juliet, both thinking the same thing – that Jay might have some information to share with them about this man who harassed Meg.

A pretty blond woman wearing a sleeveless navy dress came up to their table and sat down. "Can I join you?" Her words slurred slightly from one drink too many.

Lisa introduced her friend. "This is Lucy Millhouse. We've known each other for ages." Although Lucy was short and petite, her bare arms showed well-defined muscles that could only come from hours of working out.

Lucy shook hands and smiled, her lids drooping a bit over dark blue eyes. "Not ages, that makes us sound so old. We met in kindergarten."

Chuckling, Lisa said, "That *was* ages ago."

"Do you work at the real estate agency?" Juliet asked.

"Oh, no," Lucy said giving Lisa a teasing look, "I have a real job. I teach physical education at the high school and I teach yoga, martial arts, and weight-training on the side."

The four discussed their jobs and what they liked and didn't like about them. They voted Juliet's job as *best occupation* since she could be outside and active in every season.

"I'm active in my job," Lucy said, "but some of the kids can be a handful so it can be difficult at times."

Shelly's job was voted *best occupation for your good friend to have.*

"I wouldn't want to be a baker because I'd eat everything I made, but it would be great to have a friend who baked," Lisa told them. "All those yummy things whenever you get together." She kidded Shelly, "I bet you're very popular."

A cloud settled over Lucy's face. "I've been thinking about that poor woman. Jill Murray. I was with her the night before ... she died."

"You knew her?" Shelly was hopeful that they might learn some things about Jill.

"Not really." Lucy gave a head shake. "I was asked to show her around town. She interviewed at the high school for the open math teacher position. The interviewers were so impressed with her. They asked if I could answer Jill's questions about the school and the town, take her around, show her the sights. The committee was going through the necessary channels and doing the paperwork needed to make her an offer. They really wanted her to accept the job." Lucy rolled her eyes. "We were all hoping that Jill would accept. If she didn't, it was a pretty sure thing that the superintendent's son would get the job. Not a good idea."

"Why not?" Juliet asked.

Lucy and Lisa exchanged a look of disgust.

"Scott Bilow isn't teaching material," Lucy explained. "He's full of himself, arrogant, has a nasty temperament. He has a reputation for one-night stands, hooking up with the tourists who come to town. Not the best role model for high school students. Scott is an engineer, but he's always getting fired from his jobs. I've heard he's in big financial trouble. He only wanted the teaching position because it was something he wouldn't get fired from since his daddy was in charge of the school district." Lucy let out a sigh. "I liked Jill. She would have been a great addition to our staff." She reached for her wine glass and Shelly could see the woman's fingers shaking.

"Did Jill seem like she'd accept the job?" Juliet asked.

"I thought she might. We had fun together. I took her on the ski lift to get a view of the area. We went biking, took a hike. I showed her the crooked trees." Lucy passed her hand over her eyes. "I took her to lunch. We came here for drinks one night."

"Was that the night before she died?" Shelly asked gently.

"Yeah." Lucy's face hardened. "That stupid Scott Bilow was here. He came by and was a real pain. He'd had too much to drink ... he was leering at Jill. He told her *he* was getting the job at the high school and they only brought her in so they could prove they'd interviewed other people. Jill looked devastated. I told her that wasn't true at all. I told her the committee was going to make her an offer. Scott burst out laughing. I wanted to kill him."

"What happened?" Shelly asked, apprehension flooding her body.

"Scott put his arm around Jill and she got up so fast her drink fell off the table into his lap. He was livid." Lucy glanced at Lisa. "You know how he is, such a hot-head. Jill stormed away. Scott stood up and grabbed a napkin and tried to dry his pants. He was muttering. I couldn't understand what he was saying. I got up and told him thanks a lot for ruining a nice evening. I went to look for Jill, I even went up to her room and knocked on the door, but no one answered. I sent her a text apologizing for Scott's behavior and asking her to meet at the diner in the morning for breakfast. I didn't hear from her." Lucy swallowed hard. "I ... I never saw her again."

———

10

When Shelly got off work from the bakery, she rode her bike to the other side of the mountain to take part in an activity that Juliet had recommended to her. Shelly had never done zip-lining before, and although she was looking forward to the adventure of it, she had some trepidation about the heights involved and with being hooked to a slender cable as she flew over the woods and valleys. Juliet assured her she would love it so she swallowed her fears and signed up for the tour.

Arriving at the base lodge, Shelly met her two tour guides, Jack and Molly, and the four other people, a middle-aged couple and their two teenaged daughters, who would make up her group.

The guides provided a ground school orientation about the equipment and safety procedures and then outfitted the five of them with harnesses and helmets before heading out to the four-wheeled drive vehicle that would transport them up the mountain over fire trails through the woods. As they bumped along the wide paths, the guides discussed the area's flora and fauna, the geology of the region, and the history of the mountain range.

"So today our tour will take us on ten zip lines, three sky bridges, twenty tree platforms, and four rappels," Molly told the group as she pulled on her work gloves. "The zip lines range from ten feet off the ground to start with, until at one point, you will zip along at about thirty miles per hour and be two hundred feet above the forest floor."

Shelly felt her heart rate speed up.

Jack said, "The rappels will range from ten feet to ninety-five feet off the ground. Remember that some people have a fear of heights so we ask everyone to be supportive and encouraging to each other. No teasing or mocking, please. It's normal to feel some nervousness. Molly and I are here to ensure you have a wonderful time." He smiled broadly. "So let's get going."

One of the teenagers glanced at Shelly with a worried expression and Shelly gave her a cheery smile ... even though she was sharing the girl's concern about what they were about to do.

The sun's rays filtered down through the branches and leaves and felt warm on Shelly's face and she took some deep breaths to try and rid herself of the anxiety that picked at her.

"Are you as afraid as I am?" the dark-haired teenager whispered to Shelly.

"Probably more so." Shelly gave the girl an understanding smile.

Molly lined them up at the first zip and gave instructions about how and when to slow their ride over the cables. Each zip line became slightly higher and by the fourth trip down the cables, Shelly had gained some confidence.

The next activity required the members of the group to rappel down from one of the platforms so that they could hike to the next line. Hooked safely into place, Shelly made the mistake of looking down and her heart jumped into her throat and her vision swam.

"Don't look down," Molly encouraged. "Just step off and begin the descent."

Shelly stood frozen in place.

"Take some deep breaths," Jack suggested from below. "Keep your eyes looking slightly up and now, slip your feet slowly off the platform.

Her heart beat pounded so loudly in her ears that Shelly could barely hear the guides' helpful tips. Closing her eyes, she inched herself off the platform and moved her hands over the cable to lower herself, foot by foot, to the forest floor. When she reached the bottom, everyone applauded and praised her for meeting her fears.

Jack clapped her on the back and smiled. "It's more fun if you keep your eyes open. Next time, just peek a little."

Shelly looked up at the platform she'd descended from and felt a rush of pride that she'd been able to rappel from such a height. Although pleased with herself, she hoped the other activities would be less scary, but she wasn't holding out much hope that would be the case. Hiking to the next zip line, Shelly chatted with the family in her group.

"I didn't think I could do it," the dark-haired girl named Caitlin announced. "But when I watched Shelly, that gave me confidence that I could manage it, too."

"You're a good role model." Jack came up beside

Shelly, his bright blue eyes shining and his chestnut-colored hair falling over his eyebrows.

Shelly rolled her eyes. "I'm a chicken."

"Everyone is afraid of something. Being able to face fears is a sign of strength."

Shelly turned her head to Jack. "I bet you tell that to all the scaredy-cats."

Jack chuckled. "I do, but only some people actually listen to me. Occasionally, we have to call for help to get someone off a platform."

"Well, that was almost me today." Shelly removed her gloves to wipe her sweaty hands on her shorts. "And we're only halfway done so there's no telling what might happen next."

"I'll keep my eye on you."

Jack's smile gave Shelly a flutter. "I'll probably need that."

Molly led the group onto the next launching platform. "This one is the best zip line experience of them all."

The words sent a shiver down Shelly's back and when she stepped up onto the platform, her blood nearly froze. The cable line ran over a deep canyon and even though she knew it didn't, it seemed to go on for a mile. Bringing her hand up to her forehead,

Shelly turned away from the view and almost whimpered.

Jack noticed her reaction and said softly, "It isn't as bad as it looks. It's over in a few seconds. You can do it."

"Can I go first?" The words came out in a hoarse whisper. "If I stand here another minute, I'll pass out."

As Molly crossed the canyon before the others so she could direct the members of the group when to begin to slow their approach to the other platform, Jack moved Shelly into position to hook her harness to the cables.

"Ready?" Jack asked. "You don't have to look down, but keep your eyes open a little so you can see Molly. When it's time, she'll give you the sign to slow down." Jack squeezed Shelly's shoulder. "See you on the other side. Off you go."

Shelly was certain that her heart had stopped and as she flew over the cable high above the canyon, she kept her eyes open in slits. Halfway across, she took the risk and looked down for a few moments at the spectacular sight of the mountain range, the forest, a lake in the distance, and the blue sky stretching beyond. She quickly shifted her gaze to Molly who gave her the sign to slow and in a few seconds, Shelly had made it to the opposite platform.

Molly high-fived the young woman and when Shelly set her feet on the wooden stage encircling the tree trunk, her wobbly legs nearly gave way. Once she was unhooked from the cable, she sat down to wait for the others and her thoughts alternated between wanting to kill Juliet for suggesting the outing and thankful that she'd had such a wonderful experience. "Is that the worst one?" she asked Molly, croaking the words out.

With a laugh, Molly answered. "Yup. You've conquered the mountain zip lines. The rest of them are high, but the view isn't as dramatic so you don't feel like you're as far up."

"I guess that's comforting." Shelly kneaded her rubbery leg muscles and cheered each group member as they landed on the platform.

A man's voice called up to Molly from below. It was another zip line guide.

"What's wrong?" Molly leaned over the edge.

"Madison is coming down with a migraine. We have three clients. Can you take them with you the rest of the way? I'm going to escort Madison back down to the base lodge."

"Sure." Molly nodded. "Send them here and they can finish with us."

In a minute, three young men in their early thirties emerged from the trail and approached the tree that held the platform.

Molly greeted them. "We'll all be rappelling down and then we can go on to the next zip."

Shelly was the first to rappel down after Molly and she handled it like a pro. Molly unhooked her from the cables and Jack assisted the next person in attaching the safety hook so they could begin their descent.

Shelly said hello to the young men.

A tall, muscular guy with dark brown hair stepped over to shake Shelly's hand. "I'm glad we joined your group." He leered at her. "It was a fantastic view of your butt as you rappelled off the platform."

Shelly's face hardened as she yanked her hand from the man's grasp. "Not funny."

"It wasn't meant to be funny." The guy held her eyes and took a step closer. "It was the honest truth."

His companions chuckled.

Molly bristled. "That isn't appreciated," she said firmly.

"Oohh, sorry." The dark-haired man made a

mock-sad face. "I didn't think it was against the law to appreciate beauty."

Molly moved in front of Shelly. "It's against the rules of the zip company to be inconsiderate of other guests."

"Inconsiderate? It was a compliment." A pretend hurt expression formed over the annoyer's face. "No harm intended."

The rest of the group completed the activity and they moved along the trail to the next zip line. Shelly walked behind Molly not wanting to be near the three clowns at the back of the pack whose whispering and laughing made her feel uncomfortable. The happy mood of the group had dissipated due to the unwelcome fooling around and mocking comments of the young men.

Jack approached the guys. "I think the day of adventure has come to a close for you three. Molly will take the others to complete the course and I'll walk you down to the base lodge."

The dark-haired man pulled himself to full height and growled. "We paid for the whole course."

"You'll be reimbursed at management's discretion. You can speak to the manager as soon as you get to the lodge," Jack said calmly as he extended his arm to indicate which trail the men should follow.

"What if we don't want to end the fun?" the man asked.

Jack pulled out his small walkie-talkie-like communicator. "Then I'll have to call security."

"I've had enough of this so-called fun adventure." The man glanced over at Shelly. "Maybe you'd like to come with us? Have a drink with me down at the lodge? Get away from these adventure losers?"

Shelly's hands went clammy. "No, thanks. I'm going to finish the course."

The guy's eyebrow went up as he stared Shelly up and down. "Then another time, for sure. I'll look for you around town." He turned to Jack. "Lead the way, boy scout."

The man's companion chortled and clapped him on the shoulder. "Good one, Scott."

Shelly watched gratefully as the four men disappeared down a trail and then a worrisome thought popped into her head. "Will Jack be okay with them?"

Molly smiled. "Jack can take care of himself *and* those guys. He's a black belt in karate and ex-military. Those guys try anything, then they'll end up in pieces." She started off for the trail that would take them to one of the last zips. "Come on, everyone. Sorry for the minor disturbance."

Glad to be rid of the awful fools, Shelly started to join the others, but took a quick glance at the path the men had taken realizing her relief was tinged with a smidge of disappointment.

She was sorry to see Jack go.

11

Shelly rode her bike through town and turned onto her road, still exhilarated and proud that she'd managed her fears enough to enjoy the zip line adventure. Although she didn't know if she'd ever attempt such a thing again, she was pleased to have done it and, had to admit, was even more pleased that it was over. Passing by Juliet's cottage, Shelly noticed something on her front porch that made her apply the brakes to slow down her bike.

A man was sitting on one of her porch rockers.

Stopping, but still straddling the bicycle, Shelly's jaw dropped when the man stood up with a wide smile, a bottle of wine in one hand and a bouquet of flowers in the other. "I wondered how long I was going to have to sit here before you came home."

Tightening her grip on her bike handles, Shelly could feel the blood drain out of her head. "What? What are you doing here?" she demanded, her voice filled with anger and concern.

The man was the obnoxious person who'd joined and disrupted her group on the zip excursion.

He came down the porch steps and held the bottle slightly aloft. "I thought we could enjoy some wine together. I'm Scott." He held out his hand to shake, but Shelly ignored it.

"How did you know where I live?" Shelly pulled her pack from her back and unzipped the side pocket reaching in and wrapping her fingers around something.

"I've lived in Paxton Park my whole life. I know a lot of people." Looking smug, Scott grinned at Shelly. "I asked around."

Her eyes flashing, Shelly said, "You were rude on the mountain. You behaved immaturely. It's not something I find attractive."

"Aw, come on." Scott took a step closer, eyeing the young woman. "Most women love bad boys."

"I'm not one of them." Shelly swung her leg over her bike so that she could roll it between her and the man. "I'd also appreciate if you don't make yourself comfortable on my porch or anywhere else on my property unless invited."

"Quite the spitfire." Scott smiled broadly. "I like that."

"I don't care what you like." Shelly's blood was boiling. "I'm going inside alone and you're going to leave." As she rolled the bike forward and to the side, the man reached out and grabbed her arm to stop her.

"Back off," Shelly roared and lifted her hand which held the item she'd removed from her backpack.

"Whoa, whoa." Scott reacted to seeing the canister of pepper spray by stepping back so quickly that he practically tripped over his own feet. "No need for that." He held his hand up in a halt gesture.

The door to Juliet's house opened and a woman stepped out. "What's going on out here?" Jay's voice boomed as Juliet peeked over her sister's shoulder. "Scott Bilow, what are you doing?" The police officer stormed down the walkway.

"Officer Smyth." Scott looked almost sheepish. "I just stopped by to ask this young woman to share a drink with me."

Jay stood with her hands on her hips. "Well, she does *not* look amenable to the idea. In fact, she looks downright opposed." Glancing at Shelly, Jay asked, "Am I reading this encounter correctly?"

"You are." Still gripping the pepper spray, Shelly lowered her hand and glowered at Scott.

Juliet hurried over to stand by her friend. "Are you okay?"

"Just annoyed." Shelly's eyes flashed at the man. "For the second time today."

"It might be a good idea to make yourself scarce, Scott." Jay gave the man a hard look. "And in the future, why don't you focus on women who are actually interested in you."

Scott hesitated for a moment as if he had something to say, but reconsidered, stood straight and headed down the street at a fast pace.

"That was Scott Bilow?" Shelly was livid. "The guy who hassled Jill Murray about the teaching job?"

"Yes, that's him." Juliet watched the man hurrying away. "He's an idiot."

Jay let out a sigh. "That guy just can't stay out of trouble."

Shelly reported how Scott and his friends had joined her group on the zip line and behaved badly until one of the guides removed them from the course and took them down to the lodge.

"Sounds like Scott," Jay said with disgust. "Steer clear of him." Heading to her car parked in Juliet's driveway, she told her sister, "I'll see you on the weekend."

"You want to come in for tea or coffee?" Juliet asked her neighbor.

Shelly declined the invitation. "I want to shower and change and I have to plan the bakery items that need to be made tomorrow. Thanks for the help with Scott."

"It seemed like you had things under control." Juliet smiled. "I don't think Scott will come around again anytime soon."

Shelly rolled her eyes. "He'd better not."

The two parted ways promising to meet for a bike ride the following evening.

As Shelly climbed the steps to her front door, she could see Justice sitting on the windowsill in the living room glaring out at the rocker Scott had been sitting in. When she opened the door, the cat rushed onto the porch and made a beeline to the rocking chair. Circling it slowly, she sniffed the wood with caution. Justice made eye contact with Shelly and let out a long, low hiss.

"You can say that again," Shelly agreed and she and the cat went inside.

~

AFTER SHOWERING and having a bite to eat, Shelly sat in the easy chair intending to relax for a few minutes before planning the bakery sweets for the rest of the week. Every now and then, her annoyance and anger at Scott Bilow would flare up and she'd have to focus on slow breathing and releasing the tension in her muscles. *I won't let that man ruin the rest of my day.*

Justice settled on the young woman's lap and the combination of the cat's gentle purring and the comforting sensation of the soft fur against Shelly's hand caused her eyelids to droop until she drifted off to sleep.

A dream took shape that had Shelly flying over the forests of Paxton Park, the wind against her face, the sun warming her skin as she dipped and soared like a bird over the mountain trails. Spreading her arms like wings and taking in the natural beauty of the towering pines, the crystal blue lake, and the majestic mountain filled her heart with pure joy. When Shelly flew down over the treetops, a scream pierced her reverie and caused her to bobble in the air. She looked down to see the faces of Jill Murray and Meg Stores staring up at her, their arms outstretched reaching for her help.

In the next dream image, Shelly lay on her back gazing up at a sky almost too bright to look at. About to shield her eyes with her hand, her sister Lauren, with a gentle smile, stepped in front of her and blocked the sun's glare.

Lauren reached out and took Shelly's hand to help her stand, gestured for her to follow, and turned without speaking. They walked down the grassy hill and stopped at the edge of a wide blue lake. Lauren pointed at the glass-like surface of the water.

Tiny whirlpools began to show ... the water sucked and swirled into small circles spinning faster and faster until a rectangular portion suddenly stilled. Shelly stared at it.

The water's surface had become like a small movie screen and, on it, Shelly could see Jill Murray storming through the resort pub to the guest rooms' elevator bank. A man who looked like Scott Bilow stopped her and they exchanged what seemed to be heated words. Jill stepped into the elevator and the doors closed. The man watched the floor indicator lights above the doors as they lit up and darkened when the elevator paused on some of the hotel floors. The scene dissolved in a swirl of water and a new one took its place.

Jill ran along a wooded trail. Shelly could hear the woman's breath as she took in air and blew it out. Footsteps could be heard that didn't belong to Jill ... they got closer. Jill moved slightly to the left to allow more space for the runner behind her to pass and when the person drew near, Shelly sensed a blow to the back of the woman's head. She heard a groan as Jill crumpled to the ground.

Shelly's vision faded to black.

Feeling a damp, rough tongue on her cheek, Shelly's eyes fluttered open to see Justice's face only an inch from her own. The pink tongue licked the tip of Shelly's nose causing the young woman to smile. She wrapped the calico in her arms and brushed her cheek over the cat's velvety fur. "I miss Lauren," she whispered to the sweet cat. "I miss my sister."

Justice responded by rubbing her head against Shelly's hand, but then her ears twitched and her head lifted directing her blue eyes to the door. A low guttural sound vibrated in the cat's throat causing a burst of anxiety to flash in Shelly's chest.

Does Justice hear someone? Has Scott Bilow come back?

The feline jumped to the floor and stared at the door while Shelly pushed herself out of the easy chair and stood perfectly still, listening for any sound. The lamp by the chair was on and she wanted to flick it off, but didn't want to alert anyone that she was moving around inside.

The doorbell sounded causing Shelly to startle. She didn't want to answer and her mind raced with thoughts of what to do. If she didn't answer the door, would the person think she wasn't home and break in? She grabbed her phone from the side table in case she had to place an emergency call. The doorbell sounded again.

Moving her feet over the hardwood floor, Shelly tiptoed to the door and placed her ear against it. When a hard knock on the wood made her jerk her head up and away, she wished there was a peephole in the door.

"Shelly?" A woman's voice spoke.

Not recognizing the voice, Shelly exchanged a look with the cat and then raised her voice to ask, "Who is it?"

"It's me. Can I come in?"

With shaking hands, Shelly opened the door a crack. Her eyes widened when she saw who was standing under the porch light.

12

The glow of the golden porch light glimmered on the woman's ebony hair.

"Maria?" Shelly's surprise was evident in her tone.

"Can I come in?" Maria's shoulders drooped and there was a heaviness in her voice when she said, "I didn't think I'd be back in Paxton Park again, but here I am."

Shelly gestured to the sofa and then went to the kitchen to get some slices of cake and a pitcher of iced tea. "I was surprised you left town so quickly."

"I was overwhelmed." Maria accepted a glass of tea. "All I wanted to do was get out of here. I'd packed most of Meg's stuff into a rental van. I was going to ask the owner of the house to send me the rest of the things. There wasn't much left in the house anyway, some files, a few books. I'd had enough ... Meg's death, the person trying to break in, that note. I didn't want to spend another minute in that house. I had to get away."

"The police tried to contact you," Shelly said. "A detective came and spoke to me. I was worried something had happened to you."

An expression of remorse passed over Maria's face. "I shouldn't have left like that. I went to a friend's place and stayed a few nights. My phone stopped working and when I bought another one, I was horrified to see all the missed calls from law enforcement come up. It was irresponsible of me to rush away without informing them, but it never entered my head that the police might think something happened to me." Maria clasped her hands together and her face became serious. "They asked me to come back to town to talk to them about the fire."

Shelly handed Maria a plate with a slice of cake. "It was a shock to wake up to the house fire. I couldn't believe it. At first, I worried that you might have been inside. It was a relief when the police said the house was empty."

Maria made eye contact with Shelly and said softly, "I know they suspect me."

"The police will talk to you and eliminate you as a suspect," Shelly encouraged. "It's just standard operating procedure. You don't have to worry. Something you might tell them could lead to the person who set it."

"I talked to the police already, late this afternoon." Maria let out a sigh. "I told them I left the house, took a cab back to the hotel, checked out and drove away. I don't smoke, I didn't light any fires in the house, I didn't leave the stove on. They kept asking the same questions over and over."

"How did the meeting end?"

"It didn't end with only the talk about the fire." Maria rubbed her forehead. "After they questioned me about the blaze, they asked me about the note. I told them the same things that I told them before. I found it in Meg's file. They didn't seem to believe me."

"Why wouldn't they?"

"The police checked the paper for fingerprints." Maria lifted her eyes to Shelly. "Guess what? Mine are the only prints on the note, well, and yours since I handed you the note to look at."

Shelly's mind raced. "Well, if ours are the only prints on the note then whoever wrote it must have worn gloves."

Maria looked pained. "But Meg's prints weren't on the note either."

At first Shelly didn't grasp the importance of that fact, but then it dawned on her. "How could that be? If Meg found the note or received it somehow, she would have touched it, she would have held it. Her prints would be on it."

"Exactly." Maria leaned back. "Guess what else? I'm not supposed to leave town without telling the police."

Shelly groaned, but nagging questions about Maria's guilt or innocence began to grow and a sense of unease zipped through her nerves. "What are your thoughts about the note? You must have been thinking about it since you left the police station."

"I don't know what to think. Could Meg have spotted the note and picked it up with a tissue so as not to disturb any fingerprints that were on it? Maybe that's why hers don't show up on the paper?"

"That could be." Shelly wondered if it was likely though. She glanced over to see Justice sitting straight in the opposite chair taking in every word Maria was saying.

"The police kept asking me about the house," Maria said. "They asked if I was sure I'd heard someone at the back door. I told them that their officers saw the scratch marks indicating a potential robber. You know what they said? They asked if *I* might have caused those marks when I had trouble unlocking the door." The dark-haired woman's lips tightened into a line, and then she added, "I know what they're implying. They're suggesting that I intentionally made those marks around the door lock to *make it seem* like someone tried to break in."

"To deflect suspicion away from you and onto someone else?"

"Yes." Maria looked absent-mindedly around the room. "What a mess. My sister killed and now the police are looking at me as an arsonist. Why would I set the fire?" Her voice hardened. "Why would I do such a thing?"

Shelly thought the police might also be considering Maria as a suspect in her sister's murder, but she didn't voice that possibility to the woman. "It might be a good idea to talk to a lawyer."

Maria leaned forward with her head in her hands. "I don't know. Will that make me look guilty? Like I'm trying to defend myself because I'm guilty of setting the fire?"

"It's your right to have counsel," Shelly said. "It's not an indication of guilt."

"Huh. I bet that's not how the police will see it." Dark circles showed under the woman's eyes.

"You should talk to a lawyer anyway. I think it would be helpful." Shelly asked, "Did you know that Meg had trouble with a guy when she was working as a real estate agent back in Eastborough?"

Maria looked surprised. "She mentioned it to me."

"Did she tell you the man's name?"

"Um, I don't know. If she did, I don't recall it."

"Was she afraid of him or did she brush it off as a man just showing interest in her?"

"Meg was shook up about it initially, but she seemed to brush it off pretty quickly. She really only brought it up once over the phone. Next time we talked, I asked her about it and she said it was over and changed the subject. I didn't think about it again." Maria narrowed her eyes. "Why do you ask?"

Shelly shrugged. "Somebody mentioned it. I wondered about it."

"Meg was resilient. Nothing much bothered her."

"I know I asked before, but did you have a chance to think if Meg might have known Jill Murray?"

Maria's eyes widened. "I don't recall her ever

mentioning the woman. How would Meg know the other victim?"

"Jill was from Ashbury," Shelly said. "That's only five miles from Eastborough."

"Both women were from central Massachusetts," Maria mused. "It must be a strange coincidence." Her face seemed to relax. "You know, I've been thinking about Meg and how much she loved the outdoors. She and my parents used to come here to ski some winters. Meg was the opposite of me. I hate bugs and the summer heat and the winter cold. No way I'd spend any time on a ski slope. I'd rather read a book or go to the theatre or a museum. Funny, isn't it? How different siblings can be."

Shelly's thoughts turned to her own sister. Lauren had no patience for cooking or baking. She loved numbers and the beauty of math and would throw herself into solving long equations and problem sets. Shelly could add, subtract, multiply, and divide and she had a head for business, yet math was not her thing ... but how she enjoyed sitting quietly, watching her sister work at a board or on a long pad of paper ... it was almost as if she could see the numbers and solutions floating in and out of her sister's head. "Yeah," Shelly said, a slight smile forming over her mouth from thinking of Lauren. "Siblings can be very different."

"Thanks for listening to me rant." Maria drained the tea from her glass. "You've been nice to me and I appreciate it. I needed to talk and even though a number of people from town have been kind to me, you were the first person I thought of." She smiled. "Lucky you."

"I don't mind at all." Shelly offered more refreshments.

"Thanks, but I'm meeting someone shortly for a late dinner. Another person who has been helpful to me." Maria stood up. "Can I use your bathroom?"

Shelly pointed the way down the hall and then started to gather up the dessert plates from the coffee table. When she bent down to pick up a napkin that had fallen to the floor, Maria's phone, resting on the table, pinged with an incoming text and it caught Shelly's eye. She almost dropped the plates when she saw the name of the caller.

Scott.

Was it Scott Bilow? How would Maria know him? A flood of worry and unease raced through Shelly's veins and her heart rate sped up.

Justice let out a growl.

Maria walked down the hallway to return to the

living room. She picked up her phone, glanced at the screen, and shoved it into her bag. "Thanks again."

"Have a nice dinner." Shelly walked Maria to the door and, trying to sound nonchalant, asked, "Who are you meeting?"

"Just an acquaintance." Maria stepped outside, walked down to the sidewalk, turned and waved goodnight.

Once the front door was shut, Shelly leaned back against it and let out a sigh. The conversation she'd had with Maria swirled in her head. The note with only Maria's fingerprints on it, the attempted break-in at Meg's rental house when Maria was there, Maria's hurried departure from Paxton Park right before the fire, the fire.

Justice padded over and sat down in front of Shelly.

"What's going on? What's the answer to all of this?" Shelly asked. "What do you think, Justice?"

Justice let out a howl and Shelly's heart sank.

13

Shelly let out a curse when two eggs slipped from her hand and broke over the floor of the diner's kitchen.

Henry came over to clean them up and gave her the eye. "You feeling okay today?"

Shelly had already burned a sheet of cookies and had to throw them out.

"I'm okay. Just feeling distracted, I guess." She went to the sink for a glass of water and after taking some gulps, she told Henry about her late afternoon visitor. "So, this guy, Scott Bilow, was sitting on my porch waiting for me to get home. I was so angry by his behavior that I was honestly seeing red."

Henry's eyes darkened as his face flushed with anger. "That one." He shook his head in disgust. "Try to steer as far away from that guy as possible. He's nothing but trouble."

"That's what I hear." Shelly let out a sigh. "His ego is enormous. He's completely insufferable."

Henry said, "I don't like to gossip, but I got this information from a very good source. Scott Bilow has a gambling problem. He's in heavy financial difficulty from his gambling losses. The guy spends money like a drunken sailor, always running up his credit cards. His father bails him out every time. The old man even bought him a small house at the edge of town. Scott can't hold onto a job. He's a smart guy, but no work ethic."

Melody came in and heard what her husband was saying. "Why have a work ethic when you know your father will step in every time you're in trouble? Scott, Sr. is a good man, but he hasn't done anything for his son by being so permissive. Scott's mother died when he was a young boy and the dad raised him. Scott was wild and gave his father a hard time, that's what I heard from friends. Anyway, he's never been held to any standards and this is the result, a sullen playboy who spends his father's money like water, expects to be bailed out whenever he gets into trouble, is dismissive and rude to the people around him. It's a shame."

"That sounds like him." Shelly crossed her arms over her chest.

"He's been in trouble with the law, too." Melody gave a sigh. "He's broken into houses and stolen some items, has gotten into fights, stole a car once, had some drug issues."

"Why isn't he in jail?" Shelly huffed.

"He *has* done a little time, but he always gets out on good behavior or gets reduced sentences." Henry placed a cheese sandwich on the grill. "Too bad he can't display good behavior when he's in the general population."

"Scott dated our oldest daughter." Melody made a face.

"Really?" Shelly asked.

"In high school." Henry flipped the sandwich over with more energy than necessary.

"I can hear in your voices that something happened," Shelly said cautiously.

"We were wary even back then," Melody said. "Scott and Julia went to a carnival. They had a good time. He behaved himself. He asked her to his junior prom. Julia was a year younger. She pleaded with us to let her go and eventually wore us down. We laid the ground rules. She agreed to them."

Henry removed french fries from the cooking

basket. "So the idiot got drunk. Wrapped his car around a tree. Julia walked away with a broken arm, thank heavens that was all."

"We found out weeks later that Scott had hit Julia at the prom. He wanted to go joy riding and she didn't want to go along. He was rough with her, gave her a smack in the mouth. She didn't tell us until a few weeks had gone by. We thought her fat lip and cuts were the result of the accident."

Melody shivered at the memory. She kept her voice soft when she said, "After we found out that Scott had hit Julia, Henry went out and found him one night. Henry gave him what-for."

Shelly looked confused.

"I beat the punk up." Henry didn't look up from the grill. "I'm not proud of it, but if it happened again, I'd do the same thing."

Shelly couldn't help the smile from forming over her lips. "Did you get into trouble? Did he report you?"

"He did not," Melody said with some pride. "No one ever approached Henry about it so Scott must have kept it to himself." Narrowing her eyes and giving a little shrug, she added, "The only regret I have over the incident is that Henry didn't take me with him that night."

Shelly chuckled. "That probably would have been a surprise ... to be beaten up by your former date's father *and* mother. How did Scott interact with you when he ran into you around town?"

"He pretends not to know us." Melody grinned. "Even to this day."

"I guess he's never been a regular customer here then," Shelly kidded.

Henry snorted.

Shelly said, "If he ever bothers me again, now I know who to call."

Henry looked over to Shelly with a serious expression. "You got that right. Any time at all. You need help, you pick up the phone."

Henry's words made Shelly feel safe and protected. "Thanks," she smiled.

"So how was the rest of your evening after you got rid of Scott?" Henry placed two burgers on the grill.

"Actually, it was a little odd."

Henry and Melody turned to look at Shelly.

"I got another visitor later. Maria Stores." Shelly told them what Maria shared with her. "I want to believe what she says. I feel bad for her and for what's happened, but there's something that makes me unsure about her. I don't know how to describe it."

"I know what you mean," Melody agreed. "I found her to be gruff and abrupt. I wanted to be kind, but she gives the impression that she doesn't need anyone."

Shelly explained her worries that Maria and Scott Bilow were somehow involved with each other. "I don't mean romantically, although I wouldn't put it past Scott to have made a move on the woman. I feel distrustful of them and thinking about them together makes me nervous that they're up to no good."

The expressions on Henry's and Melody's faces were like mirror-images of concern.

"Bilow better not be behind the troubles here in town." Henry looked angry.

"Maria Stores couldn't be mixed up in the murders." Melody wrung her hands together. "She wouldn't hurt her own sister. Would she?"

Henry grumped. "Some people are capable of anything."

The diner got busy and Melody went out front to help wait tables while Henry furiously worked the grill to prepare the lunch orders. Shelly went back to her baking, her mind working on the things they'd discussed. Scott. Maria. Two dead women. She hoped the police would figure things out soon so she wouldn't have to worry anymore.

Shelly's recent dreams popped into her mind. Two of them had seemed so real that it made her uneasy. The dream of the dead young woman floating in the pond and the one where she saw and felt Jill Murray suffer a blow and fall to the ground filled her with dread.

Sweat dribbled down her back and she experienced a moment of dizziness so strong that she had to grip the edge of the counter for almost a full minute. When the sensation passed, Shelly hurried to the sink and splashed cold water onto her face. She took some deep breaths and returned to her baking.

I need to relax. I can't focus so strongly on these murders. A wave of fatigue struck her hard and she wished she could go home and take a nap, but the thought of falling asleep and having another dream filled her with apprehension ... although, the apprehension seemed to be mixed with something else. What was it? A sense of urgency?

There was something important about those dreams....

14

From the deck, Justice watched as Shelly placed the skewers of vegetables onto the grill next to the marinated chicken breasts as Juliet carried a tossed salad and a bowl of rice out to the patio table.

"Go on with the tale of the returning sister," Juliet said.

Shelly had reported Maria's unexpected appearance at her door last night and what had been said during her visit. "She was about to leave to meet someone for dinner and went to use the bathroom. While she was gone, her phone buzzed and I looked down at the screen. The text was from someone named *Scott*." Shelly let the name sink in. "Could it have been Scott Bilow?"

Juliet stared at Shelly. "Maria was meeting

someone for dinner and got a text from Scott?" A look of distaste washed over her face. "That is one busy man. What did he do? Go by the house and try to offer the grieving sister some comfort? He's unbelievable."

"We don't know if it *was* Scott Bilow." Shelly turned the chicken. "I asked who she was meeting for dinner. She's only been in town a few times so I wondered if she had a friend living here. She told me it was just an acquaintance."

"It very well could be Bilow." Juliet shook her head. "He's like lightning. He moves in on new people, visitors, people feeling like they need a friend. How does he even have the energy?"

Shelly brought the platter of chicken and vegetables to the table where she cut up some of the meat for Justice and set a small plate down for the cat. Juliet passed the salad to her friend.

"There are lots of things about Maria that make me suspicious of her."

"I feel the same," Shelly said. "That note, for one."

Juliet nodded. "Only Maria's fingerprints are on the paper? How would Meg have been able to avoid getting her prints on that thing? I don't buy that she used a tissue to pick it up."

"It seems kind of farfetched." Shelly added rice to her plate. "But on the other hand, if Maria is responsible for the note, why would she tell me only her prints are on it?"

"Maybe she's trying to get you on her side by confiding in you."

"Why does she need me on her side?" Shelly tilted her head in question.

"To vouch for her? She ran into you on the street the night of the fire. Did she do that so she'd be able to say she'd been with you, sort of an alibi? Did she see you coming down the street and then rush out with her story of someone trying to break into the house?"

As Shelly considered the idea, her jaw set. "Is she using me to cover her tracks? Is she confiding in me to have someone who will take her side, someone who can verify where she was? Have someone who can say to the police *oh, yes, she was very upset when she heard someone breaking in*."

"Why would she set the fire though?" Juliet asked.

"It must be for the reason we discussed earlier. She didn't want the police to find something."

"Why not just take whatever it was home with

her and get rid of it in New York City? Away from here?"

"Could it have been something hard to remove?"

"Like what?"

"Bloodstains?" Shelly suggested.

Justice looked up from her meal and hissed.

"Blood?" Juliet's jaw dropped and she lowered her voice. "You think Maria could be the killer? Yikes, I only had her pegged as the arsonist."

"I know, it's a ridiculous thought. Maria was in New York when Meg was killed."

Juliet raised an eyebrow. "How do we know where she was?"

Shelly's face went blank. "Well, wasn't she in New York? The police must know where she was."

"Jay doesn't share many details with me about cases. Most things are confidential to the investigations."

"But?" Shelly asked.

"But, I overheard something yesterday when I went to drop something off for her at the police station. Don't breathe a word ... for all I know, I heard it wrong." Even though Juliet knew no one was coming into the backyard, she still took a quick glance over her shoulder. "I heard my sister on the phone. I only heard a few things. But it seems like they're having trouble pinning down where Maria was the night before and on the day Meg was killed. Something about her cell phone being off and no one who is able to vouch for her whereabouts."

Shelly said, "Maria's phone was off when she left town so abruptly the night of the fire. She told me her phone wasn't working and when she finally got a new one and turned it on, she was shocked to see the messages from the police."

"Convenient, huh?" Juliet's eyes narrowed. "Or maybe, clever?"

Shelly jabbed a piece of chicken with her fork. "Maybe we're letting our imaginations run away. We could probably pick most anyone in town and make a case against them as the killer."

"Me?"

"I said *almost* anyone. Not you." Shelly smiled. "Although I don't know where you were the day Meg was killed."

"I was out of town and I have alibis."

"That's a relief," Shelly kidded. "I wouldn't want to be having dinner with a murderer."

"What about Scott Bilow?" Juliet asked. "He wanted the teaching job Jill Murray was probably going to get and he had an altercation with her in the resort pub the night before she was killed. They could have met up accidentally the next day, had another argument, Scott lost his temper, and...."

"That's possible." Shelly gave a nod. "But, if the two women are linked, which they probably are, why would Scott kill Meg? Did he even know her?"

"I'm not sure." Juliet put down her fork. "Do you get the feeling sometimes that things are right in front of us and we don't see them?"

Shelly nodded. "You think the police feel that way when they're working on a case?"

"I bet."

Shelly put her chin in her hand. "I know I've asked before, but do you think there's a connection between the women or do you think the killer chose them randomly and all they have in common is being attacked by the same man?"

"My first guess was they had a connection, but now, I'm not so sure." Juliet swirled the ice water around in her glass. "Could they have been in school together?"

"If that was the case, Maria would have known about Jill, wouldn't she?"

"Not necessarily," Juliet said. "Maria was fifteen years older than her sister. Meg might not have talked to Maria about school friends."

"Meg and Jill lived a few miles from each other

in the central part of the state. They came to Paxton Park a few months apart." Shelly tapped her chin with her finger.

"Maybe they worked together?" Juliet offered.

"Jill was a teacher, Meg was a real estate agent." Shelly started to shake her head, but then her eyes lit up. "What if there was a professional connection? Maybe Jill was a client of Meg's?"

"That's a good idea," Juliet said. "Maybe Jay knows this already, but when I see her, I'm going to tell her our idea."

"Real estate files." Shelly sat up straight. "I have a crate full of Meg's most recent real estate files."

"Let's look through them." Juliet's voice shook with excitement.

Shelly's face clouded. "Isn't it unethical to do that?"

Juliet stood up. "The woman is dead. We're trying to figure out who killed her. I think it's completely ethical to try to find the killer. Where are the files?"

As Shelly led the way inside, she pointed to the edge of the patio. "There's a loose brick right there. Don't trip on it."

They carried the box of Meg's work folders into the dining room and spread the paperwork over the top of the table. They each pulled up a seat to look through the files. Justice jumped up onto the chair next to Shelly.

After an hour of reading, Juliet looked across the table at Shelly with a wide grin. "Eureka," she said softly and pushed the open file folder across the table to her friend.

The page was a list of attendees at an open house that Meg had run at a home for sale in Eastborough. On the sheet's fourth line, the names Jill Murray and Kathy Blake were written.

Shelly lifted her eyes from the paper and smiled at Juliet. "Jill went to an open house that Meg held."

The calico meowed and swished her tail back and forth.

"Who's Kathy Blake? Her name is on the same line with Jill's," Juliet noted. "She must have been a friend of Jill's."

"If we could find her, we could ask her about Jill and Meg. What's the date of the open house?" Shelly ran her eyes over the document. "Here it is. The open house was a month before Meg moved to Paxton Park and four months before Jill came here for the interview."

"Was the open house the first time Meg and Jill met?" Juliet asked.

"If it was, was it a coincidence that they both came to town?"

"I'm going to call Jay and tell her what we found." Juliet went to the living room to get her phone and make the call to her sister. In a few minutes, she was back. "Jay wants to see it so I'm going to take a photo of the sign-in sheet and send it to her." Standing over the table, she took the picture and tapped at the phone to send it off.

After five minutes passed, a text came in and a wide smile spread over Juliet's face when she read it. "Jay says we're geniuses. She's going to track down Kathy Blake and when she finds her, she wants us to go along when she interviews the woman."

"Good," Shelly said, a determined look on her face. "A tiny step closer to figuring out what happened to Meg and Jill."

Justice let out a loud trill.

"You're right, kitty cat." Juliet winked at the feline. "Justice is a-coming."

15

As it turned out, Kathy Blake was easy to find. When Jay made a call to the Eastborough real estate agency where Meg had previously worked, she was told that Ms. Blake was a selectperson for the town. Ms. Blake offered to come to Paxton Park and the meeting was set for early in the morning at a small coffee shop just outside the city limits. When Juliet asked her sister why they weren't meeting at the police station, Jay answered cryptically that some interviews shouldn't be made public. Juliet pressed for more details, but Jay wouldn't say any more.

Kathy Blake, in her early thirties, was tall and very slender with short blond hair and intelligent brown eyes. She wore trim black slacks and a red fitted blazer. Her manner was friendly and forthcoming and when she saw the three women enter the breakfast shop, she stood and waved them over to join her in a booth.

Jay shook hands and introduced herself. "Captain Jayne Landers-Smyth." She gestured to her companions. "This is Juliet Landers and this is Michelle Taylor."

"Call me Shelly." Shelly sat down next to Kathy.

Juliet shook and took a seat next to her sister and opposite Kathy.

After some general pleasantries, Jay got down to business. "We were fortunate to find you and hope you might talk with us about Jill Murray."

"I'd be glad to." Kathy's face took on a serious expression. "I'd do anything I could to bring Jill's killer to justice."

"How did you know Jill?" Jay asked.

"Jill and I enjoyed working out. We've both done triathlons and had completed two ultra-marathons. We met a few years ago. We're both members of the same running club. I guess I should say we *were* members of the same running club." Kathy looked down at her hands for a moment. "Jill and I got along great. We became close friends."

"It came to our attention that you and Jill went to an open house a few months ago that was held by

Meg Stores," Jay said. "Did you or Jill know Meg before that day?"

"We didn't." Kathy shook her head. "That was the first time we met her."

"Did you and Jill interact much with Meg that day?"

"We had a long chat with Meg. She enjoyed athletics, too, so we had things in common. I was the one looking for a house, Jill came along with me. I liked Meg and asked if she would represent me as a buyer's agent, but she said she'd made plans to move to Paxton Park and referred me to someone else in her office. Jill asked Meg about the town and why she'd decided to move there. Meg told us that she loved the outdoors and had skied in Paxton Park as a teen. She said the town was lively and there was so much to do, no matter the season."

"Was Jill thinking of moving away from where she lived?" Jay questioned.

"Jill had recently broken up with a longtime boyfriend and was considering a move away from central Massachusetts. She wanted a change. She never thought of moving to the Berkshires. Meg talked glowingly about the area and Jill was eager to look into it."

"So she applied for the teaching job?" Shelly asked.

"First we took a ride out, did a day trip to check it out. We both loved the town ... all the shops and restaurants, the arts community, not to mention the natural beauty." Kathy chuckled. "I even considered making a move, but it wasn't realistic for me. I have my business in Eastborough, I'm a selectperson there. I was thrilled for Jill though, she was elated to find such a gorgeous place within two to three hours drive from her friends. When she found out the Paxton Park high school was looking for a math teacher, she applied immediately." Kathy frowned. "Unfortunately."

"Did Jill come to town for the job interview on her own?"

"I was planning to go with her." Kathy cleared her throat. "An emergency meeting of the select board was called though and I had to cancel the trip." Shifting her gaze to the tabletop, she said, "I can't stop thinking that things might have been different if I'd gone along. If I'd been there, maybe...."

Jay shook her head. "It's common to have such thoughts in situations like this. If only this, if only that...." Making eye contact with Kathy, Jay said sadly, "There's no way to know if things could have been altered ... perhaps, fate has plans for all of us and those plans are set in stone. You can't berate or second guess yourself."

Shelly stared at Jay. How many times had she rehashed the car accident and agonized over what small thing might have altered the outcome?

"Did you talk to Jill during her stay in town?" Jay asked.

"Every day, sometimes a few times a day, texts, phone calls." Kathy nodded. "She was happy, she told me all about the hiking trails, kayaking on the lake, how great the skiing would be in the winter. Jill even went on a zip-line tour and raved about the scenery and how much she loved it."

Shelly's attention pinged. "I recently moved to Paxton Park. I went on the zip line adventure, too. Did Jill mention who her guides were?"

Kathy's brows knitted together in thought. "It was a man and a woman. Could it have been Mary and Jack? No, wait, it was Molly and Jack. I remember because Jill said how friendly and knowledgeable they were. Molly was a marathon runner and Jack had been in the military. They invited Jill to get together for drinks that night to meet some of their friends. She went and had a great time."

"Small world," Shelly said. "Molly and Jack were my guides, too." Something about Jill zip lining with Molly and Jack nagged at her.

Juliet asked, "What happened to Meg didn't deter Jill from considering a move to town?"

"Oh, it did." Kathy's shoulders drooped. "We were out for dinner with friends one night after Meg had died. The conversation focused on whether or not moving to Paxton Park right after a woman had been murdered there was such a good idea."

"Jill decided it was safe to make the move?" Shelly asked.

"Jill really hadn't made the final decision," Kathy said. "She wanted to spend time in the area after the interview to get a feel for things. When we talked, I got the impression that she considered the murder a random happening and that it shouldn't keep her from a good opportunity. I think if she was offered the position, she would have accepted."

"Did Jill ever mention a Maria Stores?" Jay asked.

Kathy thought for a few moments. "Was she Meg's sister? No, I don't recall Jill bringing up anyone by that name."

"Did Jill mention a man named Scott Bilow?"

"He was the man being considered for the same job? Jill told me that the son of the school superintendent was vying for the same position and she was nervous that he would get it."

"Had Jill met Scott?" Shelly asked.

"I don't think so," Kathy said.

"Did Jill say anything negative about anyone she met here?" Jay wrote a few things in a small notebook. "Any little thing, no matter how inconsequential it may have seemed."

"No. Everything seemed good." Kathy took a sip from her coffee mug and when she set it down, her expression had changed slightly. "There *was* a little thing."

Three sets of eyes turned to Kathy.

"It was really nothing." Kathy waved her hand around.

"Tell us." Jay encouraged the woman with a warm tone to her voice.

"The night Jill went out for drinks with the zip line people and some of the other resort workers, she told me about someone who seemed a little put out. There was a teacher who'd been taking Jill around town, showing her the sights, bringing her to dinner. Jill said that the teacher had had quite a few drinks and her personality shifted from super friendly and helpful to acting a little jealous and annoyed."

"The teacher acted annoyed with Jill? Why?" Juliet asked.

"Jill thought that the woman had a thing for Jack. She was hanging on him and flirting with him. I guess Jack and Molly were chatting a lot with Jill and this teacher got jealous that Jack was showing so much attention to her. Jill said she sensed the teacher's jealousy and sort of extracted herself from Jack and Molly and moved to talk to some other people in the group."

"What was the teacher's name?" Shelly asked.

"It was Lucy something or other. I remember because Jill and I have a mutual friend named Lucy and Jill told me that the two women looked a lot alike except the Paxton Park Lucy was short and petite and our friend is six feet tall."

"Did Jill see Lucy again after that night?" Shelly questioned.

"Yes, she saw Lucy the next day. Jill said Lucy seemed herself, but that things seemed slightly off between them. Jill admitted that she felt a little uncomfortable about the previous night's episode." Kathy sighed. "The woman had been drinking a lot so the whole thing was best forgotten."

Unease brushed over Shelly's skin. "Was there something else that happened between them?"

Kathy shrugged a shoulder. "Lucy made a comment that rubbed Jill the wrong way."

"What did she say?" Juliet looked apprehensive.

"On her way to the restroom that night, Lucy walked past Jill and leaned in close to her. She whispered something like, *are you sure you want to move to Paxton Park?*"

16

On the drive back to town, Jay, Juliet, and Shelly discussed what they'd learned in their meeting with Kathy Blake.

"What Lucy said to Jill gave me a chill," Juliet said from the front passenger seat. "But in other circumstances, I wouldn't have given it another thought. Lucy was drunk and people's tongues loosen when they've had too much to drink. It's like saying, oh, I'm going to kill you, things like that. It doesn't mean anything."

"We didn't learn a whole lot about Jill." Shelly sat in the backseat, gripping the door handle. The short car ride brought back memories of the accident and filled Shelly with dread. "I was hoping to hear more about Jill that could point to someone or something."

"It's usually like this." Jay drove the car past wide, green meadows. "You never know when a little thing will break a case wide open. You have to talk to everyone and never overlook anything, keep digging, keep at it even when things seem hopeless."

Juliet let out a sigh. "I don't think I'm cut out for police work. Whenever I interviewed someone, I would grab onto what they said and think they were the guilty party. I'm too suspicious."

"Being suspicious is important," Jay said. "But you have to go about the process logically, move the puzzle pieces around, make sure things fit."

Juliet turned to her sister. "Why did you want to meet outside of town?"

"I don't like to broadcast new information. I like to sort through it first." Jay took a quick glance at Juliet. "You have to be careful who you trust."

"There are people at the station you don't trust?" Juliet's eyebrows raised in surprise.

"I'm careful, is all." Jay gripped the steering wheel and changed the subject. "Keep your eyes open, you two. This was an important contact that might have been overlooked and I'm grateful you uncovered it. By the way, that guy who'd been harassing Meg after he'd met her at an open house –

he has an alibi for the day of Meg's murder so he's been crossed off the list."

When Juliet and Shelly were dropped off at their houses, they stood together on the sidewalk discussing what to do next.

"When I was at Chet's market the other night, I asked him if he knew whether Meg was friendly with anyone in town. He told me he saw her in the chocolate shop sometimes talking to the blond girl who works there. I've been thinking of wandering over there. Maybe I'll go later this afternoon when I finish up at the diner."

"I can't go," Juliet said. "I have a bike tour to give at that time." She smiled. "You should be safe going by yourself."

Shelly teased, "I'll be sure to text you if the girl tries to attack me."

Before heading into her house, Juliet asked, "A group is getting together tomorrow afternoon for a bike ride on the trails. Want to come along?"

They made plans to meet at the mountain after Shelly got off work.

~

SHELLY STOPPED at home to change after finishing her shift baking in the diner's kitchen and it was nearly 5pm when she opened the door to the Main Street chocolate shop. The delicious odor of butter and sugar mixed with the smell of spices and nuts caused Shelly's mouth to water. Glass cases filled with beautiful displays of sweets lined the walls of the space. The cream-colored walls, white tile floor, high, gold-hued tin ceiling, and pewter light fixtures gave the shop an upscale, clean and cozy atmosphere. Eyeing all of the chocolates sitting in little paper and foil wrappers on glass shelves made Shelly wonder why she'd never visited the shop before.

A young woman with short blond hair came out from the backroom and greeted Shelly. Her name tag said, "Angela." Shelly admitted she was overwhelmed with the choices so the pleasant girl told her about the selections and let her sample some of the candy.

After choosing some chocolates to fill a medium-sized box, Shelly brought up the real reason she had come to the store. "You knew Meg Stores?"

Angela's face registered surprise. While she wrapped Shelly's purchase, she nodded. "I knew her."

"I live on Meg's street. I've only been in Paxton Park a short time. The deaths unnerved me."

Angela didn't say anything so Shelly went on. "I've met Meg's sister, Maria." She explained about the night Maria heard someone breaking into Meg's rental house.

Angela took a quick look at Shelly as she placed the purchase into a small, white bag.

Hoping to get Angela on her side, Shelly told her about finding Jill's body in the forest. "A friend took me to see the crooked trees and on the way back, we spotted Jill." An involuntary shiver ran down Shelly's back recalling the horror of the situation. "I wasn't sure I wanted to stay here. I wondered if I'd made a mistake moving to town."

Angela handed the bag to Shelly. "Have you made up your mind? Are you going to stay?"

"Honestly? I don't know. I guess it depends on whether the killer is caught or not." Shelly paid for the candy. "Have you lived here long?"

"I grew up here, but I've had the same thoughts you've had. I worry that it isn't safe for young women." Angela shrugged a shoulder. "I liked Meg. She was so nice. She worked part time at Chet's market and part time at the real estate office. We got together a lot. I was so shocked when...." She let her voice trail off.

Shelly nodded. "It must have been awful. It was a shock to find Jill's body, but to have someone you know murdered, well, I can't even imagine. I'm very sorry for the loss of your friend."

Angela took in a long breath and blinked fast a few times to keep tears from gathering. Another employee entered the store and said hello to Angela before heading for the backroom of the shop.

Angela looked at Shelly and made a decision. "I'm done with my shift. Would you like to grab a coffee?"

Shelly was delighted to be asked, smiled in agreement, and the two women walked to the coffee shop a block away and took seats at a small table to continue their conversation.

"The police don't seem to have any suspects," Shelly noted. "Did they talk to you? Did they ask questions about Meg?"

"They came in to see me right after it happened." Angela added some sugar to her beverage.

"Is there anyone Meg had a bad relationship with?" Shelly asked.

"No one." A cloud passed over Angela's face.

"There was someone who kept asking her out and wouldn't stop. The guy's a jerk, thinks every woman is dying to date him. Meg kept saying no and even told him she'd file a police report on him if he didn't stop bothering her. Finally, he got the hint."

"Who was it?"

"A guy who's lived in town all his life. A spoiled brat."

"Was it Scott Bilow?"

Angela's eyes widened. "Yeah, he's the one."

Shelly rolled her eyes. "I've had the misfortune of meeting him."

"Other than Scott pestering her, Meg was happy here. She was really enjoying living in town. She'd broken up with a boyfriend who took a job on the west coast. Meg didn't want to move there. She told me the relationship had been fizzling out for a while, that it wasn't the right match and that she was relieved to have a reason to end it. Meg was excited about starting fresh."

An idea popped into Shelly's mind. "Was this boyfriend angry about the breakup?"

"Oh, no. Meg said he was just as relieved as she was to end the relationship. It was a friendly parting of the ways. She'd only been here about a month when she started dating someone else. Meg was happy about life." A sad expression passed over Angela's face. "And then someone stole it all from her."

Shelly lowered her voice. "Do you have any thoughts about what might have happened?"

Angela shifted uncomfortably in her seat. "Not really."

Shelly picked up on the young woman's discomfort. "Did anything seem off? Was there anything going on that you think is concerning?"

Angela made eye contact with Shelly, then looked down at her mug. "I don't know. It's probably nothing. It's just a feeling that keeps coming into my head."

Her heart starting to pound, Shelly leaned forward. "What is it?"

"You mentioned that you've met Meg's sister."

"Yes."

"What do you think of her?" Angela questioned.

"I've only talked to her a few times, both times she was under duress. Have you met her?"

"I haven't." Angela looked out of the window. "I don't have a good impression of her."

"Why not?"

"Meg talked to me about their relationship."

Angela sighed. "Maria is about fifteen years older. She went away to college when Meg was only three. Meg said she didn't have any recollection of Maria living with them."

"A big age difference between them."

Angela hesitated, but went on. "The parents died in a private plane crash when Meg was seventeen and about to go off to college."

Shelly's eyes went wide. "I didn't know that. How awful."

"The Stores's were very wealthy." Angela repeated the words for emphasis, "Very wealthy. The parents founded the department stores called "Family Finery."

"That's *their* company?" Shelly was astounded. "Wow!"

Angela nodded. "So when the parents died, Maria was thirty-one and was named to head the funds that were left to her and Meg. Meg would receive access to her portion of the money when she turned thirty."

"That would have been next year," Shelly observed.

"Right." Angela let that fact linger in the air as she looked pointedly at Shelly.

"Oh," Shelly said.

"Meg told me that Maria was not happy with the idea of her sister getting half the fortune. When Meg brought up any questions about the money, Maria blew her off. She wouldn't talk about it. Meg had talked to a lawyer about representing her. The lawyer met with Meg shortly before she died and told her that there might be some irregularities with the funds and that he was hiring a financial investigator to look into it."

"What was the problem?"

"It was possible that the amount Meg expected was not present in the account."

"Maria spent the money?" Shelly asked.

"It might be that Maria has mismanaged and spent down the money."

"Yikes." Shelly shook her head.

"Meg told me that she was pretty sure that Maria had gotten wind that Meg had hired the attorney ... and was not happy about it." Angela's facial expression hardened.

"Did you tell the police this?"

"I told them that Meg and Maria didn't get along and that Maria was in charge of a great deal of money that Meg was about to have access to when she turned thirty." Angela rubbed the side of her face. "I don't know why I'm telling you all of this. I think the weight of it has been crushing me and I needed to unload."

Worry pulsed through Shelly's veins. "Did Meg think Maria could hurt her over this?"

Angela met Shelly's eyes and whispered, "Yes."

17

———

Shelly pointed the handle bars slightly to the left to keep her bicycle in the middle of the trail as she zoomed along under the canopy of trees behind the group of mountain bikers finishing the last half mile of the ride that would end at the resort. The rush of the wind dried the sweat on her brow and kept the heat of the late afternoon at bay. The physical exertion of climbing the mountain paths, the exhilaration of the race downhill, and the comradery of the riders had been just what Shelly needed to clear her head.

Pulling next to the bike racks set up at the base of the mountain near the resort restaurant, the riders locked their bicycles and headed to the employees' lodge to change into swimsuits for a dip in the cool lake. A raft was tethered in the middle of the water, a rope swing hung from a huge tree branch, and two water slides perched on the edge of the sand. Four of the eight riders ran to the swing and queued up to take the ride off the hill to plunge into the cold water. The other four hurried to the slides and, like little kids, yelled and squealed as they hurtled down into the lake.

Shelly enjoyed the high-spirits and fun of the four guys and the three women, including Molly, the zip line guide, she'd shared the afternoon with. All of them were employees of the resort and loved being active in the outdoors.

After the swim, the group entered the resort pub for dinner and Shelly ended up seated next to Molly and across from Juliet.

"Are you happy with the move to Paxton Park?" Molly asked Shelly as she perused the menu.

"I am. I love the area and the people I've met are great."

Molly kept her voice down. "The recent troubles haven't scared you away ... especially after finding Jill Murray's body?"

Shelly replied, "That was pretty terrible. I considered packing my bags and getting out of here, and I probably would have if Juliet wasn't my neighbor."

"She convinced you to stay and give it a chance?" Molly asked.

"It wasn't because of anything that Juliet said." Shelly gave her friend a smile. "It was more the feeling of friendship. I just kept putting off the idea of leaving."

"I've been here five years," Molly said, "and I almost decided to move away after the murders. If I was a newcomer, I'm pretty sure I would have left."

Carleen, the woman sitting next to Juliet, was a resort swim instructor. She rolled her eyes. "I've been living in town for three years and I'm on the fence about leaving. If the police don't make an arrest soon, I'm considering moving elsewhere. I look at everyone with suspicion. Standing in line behind someone, meeting new people, if a workman comes to the house, I wonder ... is he the killer?"

Molly nodded. "I have to say, the feeling of distrust and worry can simmer right under the surface."

"Living in a tourist town can be hard because there are so many people walking around who come and go." Juliet added her thoughts to the discussion. "It's like the perfect place to commit a crime because no one knows you."

One of the white water instructors spoke to Juliet

from the end of the table. "Hey, Jules, I hear your sister might be in line for a promotion."

Juliet looked confused. "I don't know what you mean."

"Police Chief," the guy named Jeff said. "I hear she's being considered for Chief of Police."

Juliet shook her head with an expression of puzzlement. "Does Jay know she's being considered?"

Everyone chuckled and the talk turned to a different topic as Juliet made eye contact with Shelly and lifted one shoulder in a shrug.

"I heard Jill Murray took one of your zip line tours," Shelly said to Molly.

"She did, yeah. Jill was easy to talk to, seemed like a nice person. We invited her to have drinks with us that night."

"She went out with you?" Shelly knew very well Jill went, but didn't want to let on that she'd heard about it.

"Yes," Molly said. "Jill was hoping to be offered the high school math position. You probably read in the news that she'd come here for an interview. Jill stayed in town for a while to see how she liked it."

"Did anything seem wrong when you were with her? Did you notice if Jill seemed upset by anything or anyone? Did she mention anything that might have been bothering her?"

"Not to me, she didn't." Molly sipped from her beer glass and set it down with a faraway look on her face. "A couple of days after being out with us, Jill was dead. Who'd ever believe that?"

Carleen, the swim instructor, leaned forward across the table. "That's why I'm thinking about moving away. Better safe than sorry."

"Carleen was out with us that night," Molly said. "We were all in a state of shock when we heard."

Shelly turned her attention to the broad-shouldered woman. "Did you notice anything that seemed off with Jill? Did she seem worried or upset about anything?"

"She seemed a little distracted as the evening went on," Carleen said. "But that doesn't mean anything. We'd all been drinking."

The food was delivered by the waitstaff and the group chatter fell quiet for a minute as they each dug into the meals.

Shelly asked Molly, "Did you happen to know Meg Stores?"

Molly set her fork down and she wiped at her mouth with her napkin. "I did know her. Meg was quiet at first, but she had a great sense of humor and was a wonderful conversationalist. That woman was smart. She knew about everything, literature, finances, politics, sports, the arts. She could discuss anything. I liked her. She seemed really happy here."

"How did you meet Meg?"

"I don't even remember. I think it was in a group thing, like this." Molly gestured to the people gathered around the table and went silent for a few moments. "The news about Meg ... that was very hard to hear."

"Did Meg have any trouble with anyone? Something minor? Anything at all?"

"I never heard a thing like that," Molly said. "I never noticed anything either. Meg seemed happy."

"Do you have a guess who might have killed them?" Juliet had been mostly listening.

"I don't know." Molly held her hands out, palms up. "I really don't. Maybe a tourist or a guy passing through town? The killer ran into them. It was probably random."

"Why stop then?" Juliet asked.

"What do you mean?" Molly questioned.

"If the killings were *random*, why would the killer stop? There's a whole town filled with young girls. Come to town, commit a crime, leave the area, but don't go too far away. Then when things settle, come back and do it again." Juliet looked from Molly to Shelly to Carleen. "Why stop killing?"

"Maybe the cops were getting too close?" Carleen offered.

"My point," Juliet said, "is that I don't think the crimes were random. I think there's a reason the killer chose these two girls. I bet he stalked them or knew where to find them. There's a reason he picked these two young women."

"And if we can figure out why," Shelly said, "then we'll narrow down who the killer might be."

"I have no idea," Molly said. "I don't even know what to base my thoughts on. I could never figure this out."

"The whole thing is such a waste." Juliet's facial muscles tugged down. "Who could be so miserable or angry that he resorts to murder?"

"Plenty of people," Carleen said.

"I hope you're kidding," Molly told the woman.

Carleen made a face. "I'm *not* kidding. Lots of people are angry at the world. Who knows what it takes to set them off?"

"Why do people like that have to take out their anger on someone who isn't even related to the person's troubles?" Molly wondered aloud.

"There's some psychiatric-word for people like

that, but it escapes me at the moment." Carleen returned her focus to her meal.

"At least Meg was happy here," Molly said. "For a little while." Shaking off her melancholy, she continued, "Meg made good friends, she liked her jobs and the house she rented, she'd been dating. She loved being active. It seemed like the perfect place for her. Things were going great."

"Until she ran into the wrong person," Juliet groaned. "It isn't right."

"Jack took Meg's death hard, too. He and Meg had been out on a couple of dates together." Molly traced the condensation on her glass with her finger.

"Meg and Jack?" Juliet asked.

Molly gave a nod. "It was new. It had only just started."

Although alarm bells sounded in Shelly's head, she didn't know what they were pointing to. "Jack seemed like a nice guy. Has he been in town long?"

"Not long, maybe six months," Molly said. "He left the military a year ago. He was Special Forces."

Special Forces? Jack.

Shelly couldn't make sense of why she felt so anxious. *What's going on?*

18

After slipping some cake pans into the oven, Shelly went out to the front room of the diner to sit with Juliet at one of the small tables. Juliet had stopped in to have breakfast before going to her job leading a white-water rafting tour. Her food was piled high on her plate and she dug into it with gusto.

"How can you eat so much food?" Shelly looked at the pile of eggs, home fries, bacon, black beans, and buttered toast on the plate in front of Juliet.

The young woman glanced up for a moment with a grin. "I work hard. I need the energy." She took a gulp of her orange juice. "You need to come on one of these rafting trips. The water isn't as powerful as in the spring, but it's still a great ride.

You should come along before the week is out. I'm afraid the river will calm down by then."

"I will. It sounds like fun." Shelly turned to look out the open window at the pine forest and she took in a long breath of fresh air. "I love the scent of the pine."

"You know what else would be fun?" Juliet gave her friend the eye. "Doing that 5K race with me on the weekend."

A frown formed on Shelly's face. "I don't know if I can do it. My leg still isn't what it was."

"You could alternate jogging and walking. Lots of people do it that way."

"I guess I could give it a try. It's for a good cause."

"The deadline is 6pm today. You can sign up online," Juliet encouraged.

Shelly rested her chin in her hand. "What did you think about what was discussed at dinner last night?"

"Everyone has an opinion about the murders." Juliet spoke with her mouth full, apologized for being gross, then finished chewing and swallowed. "But no one knows anything."

"Early on, we talked about the killer being ex-military."

"I remember." Juliet nodded. "Both women were

found strangled, fully-clothed, neither one sexually assaulted. It would take someone strong to surprise an athletic woman and strangle her."

Shelly recalled some details of the dream she'd had. "Unless...."

"Unless, what?"

"Unless the attacker struck the woman on the head first. That would probably disorient her for a few moments or even knock her out. That would result in little to no struggle by the victim."

"That's a good point," Juliet noted. "If the victim fought back, she'd have the killer's DNA under her fingernails. Meg and Jill must not have had the chance to fight back."

"So it must have been a surprise attack ... knock her out, strangle her before she can fully regain consciousness." Shelly's expression was serious. "That can't be easy to do. The attacker would have to be strong to knock someone out."

"The attacker would also have to know how to do such a thing." Juliet added, "I know you can look that stuff up on the internet, but that's not the same as actually doing it. I bet the killer had experience taking someone down. Martial arts experience? Military?"

Shelly gave a nod. "I think it would have to be

planned, too. Knowing the person's habits, which trails she walked or ran on would help the attacker figure out where to hide to keep him from being seen and that would allow him to get close to the woman quickly."

"Smart, except for one thing." Juliet scooped some egg onto her fork.

"What's that?" Shelly asked.

"Almost everyone in this town is strong and athletic so our ideas don't narrow down the field of suspects at all."

Shelly ignored the comment. "Last night, Molly said Jack was ex-military. He'd dated Meg and Jill had been on one of his zip line tours. He's only lived in Paxton Park for about six months."

"I know." Juliet groaned. "He seems like such a nice guy, though."

"Some killers are like that. They're friendly and nice and that puts people at ease and makes them unsuspecting." Shelly leaned forward. "I don't know who can be trusted and who can't. Sometimes it makes me nervous. A couple of times yesterday I looked at the guys in our group and wondered if one of them might be the killer."

Juliet let out a sigh. "I've felt the same way. A murder can sure change the atmosphere of a place."

"What about Maria and what I learned about the money?" Shelly brought up Meg's trust fund and how she would have been old enough soon to access the money. "It was millions. Maria might not have wanted to share all that with her sister. They were never close. Would Maria kill for that money?"

"People *have* and *would* kill over money," Juliet said. "There's just one problem. Say Maria did kill Meg ... why would she kill Jill?"

"There would have to be a link. We'd have to find a link between them."

"Then there's Scott Bilow." Shelly said the name like it made her mouth taste bad. "He made moves on Meg and was rejected. He didn't want Jill to get the teaching job he wanted and hassled her about it one night in the pub. And, Maria had a text message from someone named Scott. Could those two be working together? Scott's always losing his jobs, he must need money. Maria wanted the millions all to herself. Maybe they teamed up for a common purpose."

"I wouldn't trust either one of them." Juliet finished the last of the food on her plate. "I wish we were better at figuring this out. I feel obligated to help because we found Jill Murray's body."

"I feel the same way." Shelly sighed. "I had a

dream a while ago. My sister was in it. I saw Jill running on the trail by the crooked trees. I sort of felt her get hit in the head and then everything went black. I think Jill was strangled before she could regain consciousness." Shelly raised her eyes to Juliet. "It seemed real."

Juliet kept her eyes locked on her friend. "Have you had any other dreams?"

"Some."

"You should probably pay attention to them."

Shelly tilted her head in question.

"When I go to the police station to see Jay, I have a very bad and nosy habit of peaking at the paper-work on her desk." Juliet paused, then said, "I never go riffling through her stuff. If something is there and open, I've been known to take a quick glance. Anyway, I saw a report on her desk. There was a sentence that caught my eye ... it said what you just said to me, that the victim was probably uncon-scious when strangled. I don't know whether the report was on Meg or Jill."

Shelly's cheeks tinged pink with fluster. "That's a weird coincidence."

"Is it? A coincidence?" Juliet asked.

"Well, what else could it be?" Shelly's heart started to race.

"Have you ever had other dreams like that one?"

"I don't know. What are you getting at?"

"I've read about this kind of thing," Juliet said. "Some people have dreams that are like premonitions or that tell something to the dreamer. It's interesting that your sister was in the dream. I read that sometimes a relative or friend visits in a dream and shares important information with the person dreaming."

Shelly fidgeted in her seat. "That's ridiculous."

"No, it isn't. There's a word that describes this dream-type thing. I can't think of it. I'll look it up later."

"Don't bother." Shelly's breathing was coming in short, quick breaths. "That stuff is nonsense. It was only a dream. That's all it was. I thought it was interesting."

"It *is* interesting," Juliet said. "I don't think you should discount it. I've read about people getting unusual abilities after a severe trauma. You were in a serious accident. You lost your sister."

Her throat was so tight Shelly could barely speak. "It's not like that."

Juliet spoke in a soft voice and reached across the table to touch Shelly's hand for a second. "Your sister might be looking out for you." With a kind smile,

Juliet stood up. "If I don't get to work, those rafts will leave without me. See you later."

Shelly nodded and, even though she knew it wasn't possible, she had to blink back tears from thinking that her dear sister, Lauren, was near and was watching over her.

19

The day of the fun run dawned pleasantly warm and clear, perfect for the activities sponsored by the Paxton Park resort. In addition to the 5K run, there would be free use of kayaks and canoes on the lake, free bike tours of the area, guided hikes around the mountain, music, and food. On the way out to meet Juliet, Shelly caught a look at herself in the full-length mirror. In her running shorts, the leg scars from the accident and subsequent surgeries showed red and angry against the lightly-tanned skin. Still self-conscious about the discolored marks of damage, she rubbed her hand over one of them and felt the smooth, raised skin beneath her fingers.

Shelly parked her bike in the employee section of the resort property and found Juliet standing with a group of young men and women readying themselves for the short race. The grounds of the resort swarmed with tourists and locals soaking up the festive atmosphere of bands playing music and food vendors set up next to craftspeople selling their wares at tables and booths. People stood in line to take the ski lift ride up and down the mountain and to try out kayaks and canoes.

"This is great." Shelly had a wide smile on her face. "So many people."

"They do this four times a year, spring, summer, fall, and winter. It's good advertising for the resort." Juliet pointed. "Down that way, there are archery, skeet shooting, and martial arts demonstrations and then people get to try the activities for free."

The group headed to the sign-in table to get their numbers and then moved to the starting line with the other participants.

"I'm nervous." Shelly rubbed her palms against her shorts. "I hope I don't look foolish when I have to walk."

Juliet put her arm around Shelly's shoulders and squeezed. "You'll be fine. Look at what you've accomplished not even a year from the accident. I'll stay with you."

"No, don't. You run." Shelly knew that Juliet had

a friendly rivalry going with some of the other runners and she wanted her friend to do her best. "I'll meet up with you at the finish." She gave a little push to Juliet. "Go up front where you belong and give 'em all heck."

Prior to the accident, Shelly had been a good runner having completed five marathons. As she rubbed her thigh and calf muscles, her emotions mixed together with equal parts regret, sadness, and a tinge of anger at the loss of her physical strength and stamina. She swallowed hard trying to push the negative feelings from her mind, determined to fully recover one day.

The gun fired and the runners were off, moving slowly at first as the crowd began to separate from one another. Shelly jogged the first quarter mile and then eased to a limping walk when her leg tired. A man ran past on her left, noticed her, and stopped to walk alongside.

"Are you okay?" Jack from the zip line course asked, concern etched on his face.

"Yeah, thanks." Shelly smiled and explained her leg injury and how she was trying to get back in shape.

"I'm very sorry about the accident." Jack's tone was sincere. "I can tell that you're mentally strong.

You'll be fine. It just takes time. Be good to yourself, don't push too hard. You'll recover quicker that way."

"Do you have medical training?" Shelly asked.

"Not at all." Jack shook his head. "I've had an injury myself and I was in Afghanistan and Iraq. I saw some of my buddies wounded and watched their recoveries. You'll get better. Keep positive and give it time."

"Thanks for stopping." Shelly encouraged Jack to go ahead and run, but he declined.

"Nah. I'll walk with you. We can talk."

Although Shelly's initial sense of Jack was that he was friendly and kind, she wasn't able to shake the itch of worry that he might be the killer. She couldn't help but like the man and hated to harbor suspicions about him. The two chatted as they walked, sharing information about where they grew up, their occupations, love of the outdoors and being active, and why they made the move to the mountain. Shelly glossed over the details of the accident saying only that there had been fatalities. Jack was sensitive and thoughtful in his reaction.

Shelly said, "So I thought it was a good time to make a move and there was an opening at the resort for a baker. I like working in the kitchen with Henry.

He's a good person and fun to be around. It's part time right now which suits me fine."

"After leaving active duty, I felt like I needed somewhere peaceful and not hectic like a city." Jack chuckled. "I know this place can be crawling with tourists, but the atmosphere is happy and relaxed since most people are on vacation."

They walked without speaking for a few minutes and then Jack said, "The murders hit me hard. I went out a couple of times with Meg Stores. It wasn't anything serious, but her murder sucker-punched me. She was a nice person. I've been in war, been on missions. I lost friends. When you're home and away from such things, well, it hits hard. Things like that aren't supposed to happen at home. I couldn't believe it."

Shelly murmured understanding words. "I heard Jill Murray had been on one of the zip line excursions with you as a guide."

"Yeah, when I heard that she'd died, too, it was another shock. I wish the cops would solve this mess."

Shelly said softly, "Did you know I was one of the people who found Jill's body?"

Jack stopped walking and turned to face Shelly.

"You found her?" He blew out a long sigh and touched her shoulder. "I'm sorry."

Shelly gave a wistful smile. "How about we talk about happier things?"

"Good idea." Jack met her smile with his own and his kind, intelligent face warmed Shelly's heart.

By the time they crossed the finish line, the two young people were talking animatedly and laughing together.

"I was concerned about doing this." Shelly limped to a bench and sat down to massage her sore limb. "But, you made it fun and I forgot all about worrying about my leg."

"I enjoyed it, too. Thanks for being my 5k buddy." Jack sat down next to her. "What's your plan for the rest of day?"

Shelly undid her long braid and let her hair loose. "I'm going to meet up with a few friends, have lunch, maybe try out some of the activities. I'd like to try the archery." Shelly was about to ask Jack if he'd like to join them when he said, "Would you mind if I tagged along?"

"I wouldn't mind at all." A bright smile spread over Shelly's face.

Jack got up and brought back two water bottles, one of which he handed to Shelly. The sun warmed them as they sat on the bench listening to the music and watching the people walking around the grounds. Juliet and her friend, Fred, found them and they scrunched together to make room for them to sit.

"How did you do on the race?" Shelly asked her friend.

A wicked grin showed on Juliet's face. "I won."

"By a mile, too," Fred said.

While giving congratulations, Shelly noticed someone glaring in her direction from the other side of the main outdoor plaza. Lucy Millhouse, the blond, athletic high school physical education teacher who had been jealous over Jill Murray's interactions with Jack stood next to a concession stand holding several quivers of bows and arrows. It only took a second, but Lucy's eyes bore into Shelly's with a look of fury and disgust before she gathered up the equipment and stormed away. The hostile gaze sent a shiver of anxiety through Shelly's body.

"Shelly?" Juliet asked.

Shelly blinked and turned back to her friends. "What did you say?"

"We thought we'd head to the grill and buy lunch, then take it down to eat by the lake. I have a blanket in my car we can spread out. Sound okay with you?"

Standing up, Shelly smiled. "Sounds perfect."

Heading down to buy their food, Shelly took a quick glance over her shoulder to catch a glimpse of Lucy weaving her way through the crowd towards the field where the archery was being held.

Shelly's stomach clenched and she thought that if Lucy was involved with the archery activity, it might be a good idea to try some other event in the afternoon and completely avoid the bow and arrow demonstration. After the dirty look she'd just received from Lucy, Shelly thought it best to sidestep the woman, especially when she was around weapons.

20

After lunch, Fred and Jack got texts from resort management asking them to help out at the lake so they excused themselves and told Shelly and Juliet that they would find them later in the day. Two other friends came to join the girls and everyone but Shelly wanted to try the archery so despite maneuvering to avoid the activity and being unable to come up with reasons to do something different, she trudged down the hill along with the others.

Lucy, wearing little shorts and a tight, red tank top with the resort logo printed across her chest, finished up with a client and called, *Who's next*, as she turned around to see Shelly, the first person waiting in the line.

Shelly's heart dropped, but Lucy gave a big smile and waved her forward. "Hi, Shelly. Nice to see you."

Thrown off by the young woman's friendliness and thinking for a second that she might have imagined the earlier nasty gaze, Shelly braced when Lucy leaned close. "I saw Fred sitting with you on the bench a while ago. He was supposed to be working the archery, but he claimed he had a conflict so I got this assignment. I'm supposed to be teaching the mixed martial arts. Fred is not my favorite person at the moment."

Shelly breathed a sigh of relief when she realized Lucy's evil eye had been directed at Fred and not at her. Lucy explained the mechanics and physics of the bow and arrow and took two demonstrating shots at the red and white target. Both of the arrows hit nearly dead center.

"Impressive," Shelly said.

Lucy shrugged a tanned, muscular shoulder. "I've had a lot of practice." She took hold of Shelly's arm and positioned her body for the best aim. Handing her the bow and arrow, she went through the proper way to stand and hold the equipment. "Go ahead. Give it a shot."

Shelly steadied herself, let go, and the arrow flew

through the air to hit the uppermost part of the target.

"Great," Lucy told her. "You're a natural. Most people can't hit the target at all on their first attempt." Getting Shelly ready for another try, Lucy asked, "Where's Jack? He was with you earlier, wasn't he?"

"He was asked to work at the lake for an hour to cover lunch breaks."

"Is he joining you after that?"

Shelly thought Lucy's voice had an edge to it. "He said he might." She released the arrow and this time it hit closer to the bullseye.

"He must like you." Lucy smiled, but Shelly got the impression it was forced. "Well, nicely done. Time for the next person. See you later." Shelly was dismissed and as she walked out of the cordoned off archery space to wait for Juliet and the others to complete their turns, a man further down the line caught her attention.

The man whooped and hollered each time he tried the bow and arrow. His behavior was over the top and inappropriate and when a security guard came forward to speak with him, he adjusted his position which made his face visible to Shelly. She wasn't surprised to see it was Scott Bilow. Scott exited the area at the security guard's request and headed in Shelly's direction. When he saw her, his face lit up and he hurried over.

Without even saying hello, he boasted, "Did you see how great I was at archery? I've never tried it before. This was my first time." He seemed slightly manic.

"Good for you." Shelly kept her voice even.

Scott stepped closer. "Did you try it? I bet you're good at it, too."

Shelly could smell alcohol on the man's breath. "I had a turn already."

"Good." Scott's words slurred a little as he gestured to the resort restaurant. "Join me inside. We can get a drink."

"I don't like to drink during the day." Shelly took a tiny step back.

"Still holding a grudge against me for showing up at your house announced?" Scott made a pouty face.

"I don't bear grudges," Shelly told him.

"Look, we got off on the wrong foot. Let's start over." Scott's eyes had a glassy appearance.

Shelly looked at Scott and asked, "Do you know Maria Stores?"

Something flickered over the man's face and he seemed about to deny knowing Maria, but thought better of it. "Who did you say?"

"Maria Stores. Meg Stores' sister."

"Oh. Yeah." Scott shifted his focus to the ground. "I guess I met her once or twice."

"Is she here? I thought I saw her this morning before the race," Shelly fibbed.

"I don't know. I haven't seen her." Scott looked clearly uneasy.

"Is she still in town?"

"I think so."

Shelly watched the man's face. "I haven't seen her in a few days. I have a box of hers, it has some of Meg's things in it. I didn't want Maria to forget I still have it. Have you seen her lately?"

"What? No." Scott moved a few steps away to put distance between them.

"Is Maria staying at the resort hotel?"

"I think so."

Shelly took a chance making the next statement. "I saw you having dinner with Maria the other night."

A look of surprise passed over Scott's face and he mumbled a few words about to deny having been with Maria, but then said, "I ran into her. I wasn't having dinner with her. I sat down at her table for a little while." He narrowed his eyes at Shelly. "I didn't see you there."

Shelly had no idea where Scott and Maria had met for dinner and she froze for a second, afraid he would ask her something that would reveal her claim of seeing them together was a lie. "I ran in for a minute. I realized I was at the wrong place."

"Who were you looking for?" Scott asked.

"An acquaintance." Shelly craned her neck looking for Juliet.

"Maybe you'd like to meet *me* for dinner sometime." Scott leered at her.

Shelly kept her attention on the people in the archery area. "We've already been through this. It's not a good idea."

"I get it." Scott's expression darkened. "You think you're too good for me?"

"We're not the right match." Shelly watched him in her peripheral vision. She didn't like the tone in his voice.

"I have a master's degree, you know. I make a lot of money." Scott moved closer.

Shelly didn't reply, but she clenched her fist just in case.

"I'm smart. I know how to treat women. I can show you a good time."

Shelly flicked her eyes to the man. "I've recently come off a relationship," she fibbed. "It's not the right time for me to start something new."

"It doesn't have to be a relationship." Scott's smile was creepy. "It can be for fun."

"I don't think so." Shelly wished he would go away and leave her alone and she was glad she was in a crowd of people and not in some isolated place with him.

"You should give me a chance," Scott whined.

Shelly tried to think of something to say that wouldn't incite the man.

Scott began to amble away and as he went, he muttered, "You know what happens to girls who won't give me a chance...."

Shelly's heart jumped into her throat.

SITTING at the kitchen table leaning over a bowl of soup, Shelly spooned the warm broth with vegetables and rice into her mouth. She'd arrived home an hour ago, showered, changed into a t-shirt and shorts, and heated up her dinner. Justice was perched on the seat next to Shelly listening to the woman's monologue about the day. "And then he said, *'you know what happens to girls who don't give me a chance'*. I could barely breathe."

The calico cat hissed her disapproval.

As soon as she and her friend had a minute alone at the resort, Shelly reported her interaction with Scott Bilow to Juliet. Shocked and unnerved by the man's comment, Juliet said she would call Jay to tell her what Scott had muttered as he walked away from Shelly at the archery event. Even though she was on edge and distracted, Shelly stayed with the group of friends until late evening to kayak, hike, and listen to the outdoor concert. Jack wasn't seen again for the rest of the day.

Fred and Juliet decided to have dinner and drinks at the pub, but Shelly begged off and went home. The majority of the day had been fun and she was glad she'd done the race even if she walked most of the way. It was the beginning of what she hoped would be a full recovery of her athletic ability, and even if she couldn't manage to return to her former skill level, Shelly decided she'd work hard to be as good as she could be and would be content with that.

Despite all the fun she'd had at the resort festivities, a small part of the day's experience still picked at her. Lucy's passive-aggressive behavior and Scott's oddly threatening mutterings had put a damper on things and she couldn't shake off the feelings of unease.

After giving it some thought, Shelly had decided that Lucy probably was angry that Jack was having a good time with a group of people that didn't include her and had made up the story about being annoyed with Fred to deflect from the real reason for her irritation. Why was Lucy so jealous? If Jack wasn't interested in her, why didn't she just move on? There seemed to be plenty of eligible men in Paxton Park.

Shelly yawned and felt like crawling into her bed and pulling up the soft blankets, but her muscles ached and buzzed from too much activity and she knew she wouldn't be able to fall asleep. "How about we watch a movie together, Justice?"

The cat, standing in the chair and frozen like a statue, stared from the kitchen to the living room, its fur bristled up over her neck and shoulders.

A zap of fear rushed through Shelly's body and she sat stock still, listening, the air thick with tension as she strained to hear. After a full minute had passed, she began to relax and was about to say something to the cat when she heard a scuff and a thud that sounded like it came from the front of the house.

Shelly jumped to her feet.

What was that? Is someone out there?

21

Her eyes darting around the kitchen trying to locate her phone, Shelly realized she'd left it in the bedroom. When Justice leapt from the seat and dashed into the living room, Shelly reluctantly followed, inching down the short hallway. Stepping over the threshold into the living room, the doorbell sounded and the young woman's heart jumped into her throat.

"Who is it?" Shelly demanded, her voice loud.

"It's me. Jack Graham."

As Shelly hurried to open the front door, relief flooded her body when she saw Jack standing on the porch with a warm smile lighting up his face.

"Hi," he grinned. Glancing down, he noticed Justice at Shelly's feet and bent to greet the animal. "What a handsome cat."

Justice purred and offered both of her cheeks to the man for a scratch.

"Sorry to stop by unannounced. I hope I'm not interrupting."

"No, it's fine."

"I got called away to the zip line today at the festival. A client froze in fear in the middle of the course and it took some doing to get him down. It happens on occasion. They asked if I could go up and take over the rest of the group."

"The poor client. I completely understand." Shelly chuckled. "There were a couple of spots on the course where I panicked and thought I'd be stuck there forever."

"It can be a challenge," Jack replied. "So I wanted you to know why I didn't join up with you and Juliet and Fred later in the day." When he made eye contact with Shelly, a tingling warmth spread through her veins. Jack added, "I didn't want you to think I stood you up or anything."

"That's nice of you." Shelly felt her face flush.

Jack said, "I gave a friend a ride home. Rob Whitaker. He lives on the next street over. We were talking about the neighborhood and he told me you and Juliet lived over here. That's how I knew which house was yours."

Shelly gave a nod. "Um, would you like to come in? Have some tea or coffee?"

"Oh, no, thanks. I should get home. I need to be up early for work." Jack shoved his hands into his pockets and he nervously shifted his feet. His words came out in a torrent. "Tomorrow is supposed to be nice. If you're free in the afternoon, I wondered if you'd like to go on a bike ride. There are some great trails on the east side of the mountain I can show you."

Shelly's heart did a little flip and she tried to modulate the excitement she felt so it wouldn't be so obvious when she replied. "I finish work around 2:30pm tomorrow. I'd love to bike."

Justice trilled and rubbed against the man's ankles.

Jack's eyes brightened. "Great. Meet at the resort around 3pm then?"

"Sounds good."

Jack went down the steps to his car. "See you tomorrow afternoon."

When Shelly shut the door, she looked down at the cat with a wide smile. "I wasn't expecting that." The chat with Jack had soothed the nervous tension she'd been feeling and her mind and muscles felt more relaxed as she flicked on a movie and snuggled with Justice on the sofa.

Pulling a soft blanket over her legs, her eyelids grew heavy as she patted the sweet cat curled on her lap and thought about the day's happenings. Even though she'd walked most of it, the race had been a mental success for her and she'd enjoyed Jack's company as they completed the course together.

Jack's arrival on her doorstep was a pleasant surprise and she looked forward to the next day's bike ride with him. Her thoughts turned to Lucy Millhouse and her obvious jealousy over Jack. From what she'd heard and seen, Lucy seemed to have an obsession with the man and allowed a nasty side of her personality to flare up whenever she saw him enjoying the company of other people.

The offensive comments Lucy had made to Jill Murray about was she sure she wanted to move to Paxton Park showed the woman's deep resentment towards anyone who even casually conversed with Jack. Shelly hoped Lucy didn't find out about her and Jack's upcoming bike ride.

Thinking about Lucy's odd behavior caused her interaction with Scott Bilow to pop into her head. Scott certainly seemed like a troubled man ... unable to keep a job, always after women, boastful and insensitive to other people's wants, possessing an inflated ego. When she remembered his mutterings about what happens to women who don't give him a chance, a cold chill ran over her skin. She didn't want anything to do with the man and would avoid him at all costs.

Justice moved to rest on Shelly's chest and watching the cat for a few minutes as she rose and fell slightly with each of the woman's breaths, Shelly's heavy eyelids closed and she dozed off.

Dream images moved through her mind like shadows. Some stayed longer than others. Flying along the zip line, biking down the mountain trails, swimming in the cool, refreshing water of the clear lake.

The scent of the pine forest floated past her nostrils and the warm breeze brushed over her skin. Some oak leaves rustled overhead. A cardinal's call danced in the air and a fly buzzed near to her ear.

Her sister, Lauren, stood in the shade of the tall oak facing her.

Shelly heard running footsteps, rhythmic and even. Jill Murray, her hair pulled up in a ponytail, moved over the path, her arms pumping and her stride sure and strong. A sheen of sweat glistened on Jill's skin. Her breathing was steady. For a few moments, Shelly took Jill's perspective and saw what the woman saw as she sprinted along the trail.

Something caught Jill's foot and caused her to stumble.

A blow to the back of the head. Her vision going black.

Shelly returned to her own perspective and out of the corner of her eye, she saw the shadow of someone lunge at Jill. As the attacker's face was about to emerge from the shadow, the person's stench of fury and hate filled the air and gagged Shelly. She crumpled to the ground unable to make out the person's features.

With sweat beading on her forehead, Shelly woke up coughing and dry-heaving. Pushing the blanket off of her legs, she jumped from her seat. Justice stood on the arm of the sofa with her ears pricked forward.

Disoriented from her nap, a loud knock banged on the front door startling Shelly. She rubbed at her temple and pushed her hair from her eyes as she hurried to open the door thinking that Jack had returned for some reason.

Turning the lock and pulling at the door, Shelly's face froze when she recognized the person standing there in the dark.

Scott Bilow.

Her heart hammering, Shelly attempted to slam the door, but Scott rammed his boot between it and the jamb to keep it from closing. "Hold on," he growled.

Stumbling back, Shelly yelled. "I told you never to come here."

"Don't act hysterical." Scott entered the room. His facial muscles drooped and his eyes still had a glazed look to them. "I hate hysterical women."

Justice moved forward and released a low, menacing hiss.

Scott's face hardened and when stepped towards the cat, Shelly moved between them and glared. "This is my home. You do not have permission to be here." Despite her stomach in a knot, she pretended not to be frightened, pointed at the door, and snarled, "Get out."

"Just wait a minute." Scott's eyes blazed. "I don't want anything to do with you. Listen to me for a second. Marie Stores asked me to come by."

"What? It's late. It couldn't wait until morning?" Shelly didn't really know what time it was. "You come to my house unannounced. We aren't exactly friends. You barge your way in here. You trespass. Two women have been killed in this town. I have a right to be upset." Shelly's anger made her feel almost manic. Her head started to spin. She advanced two steps. "Remove yourself from my home before I call the police and press charges. Get back outside on the porch. You can tell me what you want from there."

Scott hesitated, his mouth twisted in a grimace.

"Go!"

Muttering curses, Scott yanked open the door with such force that it smacked against the wall. Once on the porch, he wheeled around. "Okay, I'm outside."

"What do you want?" Shelly seethed.

"Maria asked me to come by and pick up the box she left with you." Scott practically spit the words out. Even in the faint light, Shelly could see Scott's face was flushed.

"Why did she?" Shelly looked at the man with suspicion.

"What's that supposed to mean?"

"Why did she ask you to do that? Why didn't she come here herself?"

A hateful look washed over Scott's face. "Maria doesn't feel good."

Shelly moved her hand to pull the door closer. She moved her finger to flick the bolt on the knob into position so when she slammed it, it would lock. "Go home. Tomorrow I'll bring the box to the police station. You can go there to get it."

Scott was about to protest, but with one swift motion Shelly slammed the door in his face. Scott screeched his annoyance for several seconds, gave the door a hard kick with his foot and cursed, but he left the porch, got into his car, and shot away down the street.

With a growl, Justice leapt onto the table in front of the window and peered out past the gauzy, white curtains into the darkness.

"Idiot. Who does he think he is?" Shaking, Shelly leaned her back against the door and slowly slid down to the floor where she pulled her knees close, rested her head against them, and sobbed.

22

Once she'd recovered from her breakdown, Shelly called the police to report Scott Bilow's intrusion and for an hour after the fool had left, she paced around the house ranting about the man's behavior while Justice perched on the back of the sofa watching her. If it wasn't so late, she would have grabbed her bike and zoomed around town to burn off her edginess.

Shelly picked up her phone more than once to text Juliet, but each time decided against it due to the lateness of the hour. During one pass of her pacing route around the living room, she'd looked out the window to her friend's house hoping to see a light on, but the place was in darkness and she didn't want to disturb Juliet since Scott had left and no harm had been done ... except to Shelly's nervous system.

After warming some milk on the stove, she gave a saucer to Justice and then sipped from her cup while she tried to calm her breathing and push the awful man's visit from her mind. By the time she finished her drink, exhaustion hit Shelly hard from the rush of adrenaline that had exploded through her body. Feeling weak and shaky, she headed to her bed and as soon as her head touched the pillow, she was out like a light.

Early the next morning, while Shelly was tying the crate filled with Meg Stores's real estate files to the back of her bike with bungee cords, Juliet poked her head out of her door. "Why are you up and leaving the house so early?" When she saw the look on Shelly's face, she hurried outside in her pajamas. "What happened?"

Shelly gave her friend the condensed version of the previous night's event.

Juliet's eyes widened at the tale and she stood staring.

"Why are you looking at me like that?"

"I'm afraid." Juliet's fingers trembled as she pushed a strand of hair out of her face.

"Of Scott?"

"Yes. What's wrong with him? How can he be so dense to just barge into your house like that? It makes me nervous." Juliet wrapped her arms around herself. "It sounds like he's gone crazy. What if he comes back? You want to sleep at my house tonight?"

A quiver of fear raced through Shelly's chest and then her face hardened. "He better not come back or I *will* press charges."

"Stay here tonight," Juliet urged. "Just in case. It would make me feel better."

"It'll be okay. I'll keep my phone near. If he comes back, I'll text you right away."

"Make sure you do." Juliet bit her lower lip. "I don't like this. I don't like it one bit. I won't sleep a wink tonight." She convinced Shelly to put the box in her car and she'd deliver it to the police department on her way to work.

"There was some good news." Shelly grinned after putting the box on the backseat of her friend's car and she told Juliet about Jack dropping by and inviting her to go on a bike ride.

"Well, well." Juliet gave Shelly a playful poke on the arm. "I thought he was interested in you when we were all together yesterday."

"You did not." Shelly shook her head.

"I most certainly did. I saw the way his face lit up every time he talked to you."

After some more bantering back and forth, Shelly rode to work on her bike and spent the day baking and chatting with Henry and Melody. Tired of talking about it, she didn't tell the couple about her late night visitor deciding to report that news another day. The calming nature of the baking tasks along with joking around with Henry, took Shelly's mind off of Scott Bilow and when she left the diner's kitchen for the day, her mood had lightened. When she saw Jack standing next to his bike waiting for her outside, every negative thing she'd been thinking about vanished from her mind.

The two followed the base trails around the mountain to the east side where they began their ascent up the winding paths through dense tree growth, past meadows and rocky cliffs, all the way to the summit.

"The view is spectacular." Her hair damp with sweat, Shelly removed the bike helmet and pushed the wet strands off of her forehead. When she and Jack sat down on a stone wall to rest and enjoy the scenery, he indicated points of interest off in the distance.

"The mountain range continues in both directions," he said and then gestured to a large lake on the west side and to some church steeples peeking out from the foliage and he told his companion the names of the towns they were in."

"It's beautiful here, so peaceful." A contented expression showed on Shelly's face.

"Isn't it?" Jack took off his helmet and placed it on the stone wall next to him. "At least it was until recently."

They talked about how the murders had impacted the townspeople and how a sense of unease permeated so many interactions with others.

"You knew Meg well?" Shelly asked.

"Not really." Jack rubbed a knot in his shoulder. "We went on two dates and both realized we didn't share a spark. We were more like brother and sister. She and I laughed about it. We had fun together so we hung out sometimes. There was something about Meg that made me feel like I was her older sibling. I don't have any sisters or brothers." Jack gave a shrug and looked down at his hands. "I felt like I should have been able to protect her."

Shelly spoke softly. "I think that's a normal feeling when you lose a sister or someone who feels like a sister." She shared the story of the accident and losing Lauren. "Sometimes I wonder if there was anything I could have done that day that would have avoided the accident. Deep down, I know there isn't, but I just can't help thinking that way once in a while."

Jack wrapped her in a hug and held her for a few moments. "Things can't be easy can they?" He looked at her wistfully.

Shelly gave a little smile. "Some things are." Talking to Jack was one of them.

When the sun lowered towards the horizon painting the sky in sweeps of violet and pink, Shelly and Jack started to shiver from sitting so long in sweaty clothes and decided to head back. The journey down the mountain paths was a lot faster than the effort of climbing the hills and they reached the resort in no time. Before parting ways, they chatted about riding again later in the week and then Shelly and Jack headed off in the direction of their homes.

Neither one noticed Lucy Millhouse standing on the deck of the pub glaring at them.

~

JULIET AND SHELLY curled up on the sofa with take-out food and talked about their days. Justice squished in between them. Mostly the talk consisted of Juliet asking a million questions about Shelly's date with Jack.

"It wasn't a date," Shelly protested while spooning fried rice onto her plate. "We're becoming friends."

"I think you're going to become more than friends." Juliet bit into an egg roll.

"Jack's nice to be with. We'll see. I'm in no rush."

"Well, I am. I haven't been to a wedding in forever."

"You're going to have a long wait for that." Shelly bopped her friend on the arm. "Unless you find a guy, then the wedding can be yours."

After the meal and a movie, Juliet stretched and yawned. "Time for bed." She gave Shelly a serious look. "Come and stay at my house tonight."

Shelly hesitated for a second, but then said, "I don't want to be driven out of my home because of Scott Bilow. I don't think he'll come back. He *did* leave when I told him to."

"Are you sure? Shall I stay here with you?"

Shelly cocked her head. "Then Scott can attack both of us."

"No, thanks. I'm going home." Juliet stood up. "Please come."

"I'm okay, but thanks." Shelly walked Juliet to the door where they hugged goodbye.

"You call me if you need me. I don't care what time it is."

"I will." Shelly gave a nod and when Justice rubbed against her legs, she added, "The cat will protect me."

"Be sure you do," Juliet told the calico.

Shelly cleaned up, changed into pajama shorts and a tank top, put her phone on the bedside table, and climbed under the covers with the cat leaning comfortably against the other pillow. For a second, a wave of anxiety washed over Shelly. She swallowed hard, told herself not to be a such a worry-wart, turned out the light, and closed her eyes.

Two hours later, in a state of deep sleep, Shelly didn't hear the click of the back doorknob as it turned.

23

Justice touched her paw to Shelly's nose causing the young woman to stir from her slumber. When she was about to say something to the cat, Justice placed her paw on Shelly's lips and let the lowest of growls rumble deep in her throat for only a second.

Shelly held her breath and didn't move. She listened.

A creak from the wood floor.

Adrenaline shot through her body. Her thoughts raced. The house was small. How many seconds did she have before the intruder found her?

Moving the covers back, she slipped from the bed, slowly took the phone from the side table being careful not to make a sound, and stood in the darkness of the room thinking.

If I try to go out the window, it will make noise and I might not make it.

She pushed the letters on the phone and sent a text to Juliet. *I think someone's in my house. Call 911.* She worried Juliet wouldn't hear the ping of the incoming message.

A weapon. What can I use for a weapon? She berated herself for leaving the pepper spray in her backpack in the living room.

Another creak on the hardwood floor.

Scott Bilow. How dare he come back. Fury began to mix with her fear. It coursed through her veins.

Hurrying, Shelly bent and unplugged the cord to the bed side metal lamp. She lifted it. The base was round and had some heft to it. The body was slim with the diameter of a two-inch pipe. She unscrewed the finial, removed the shade, wrapped the cord around the base, moved silently to the wall, pressed her back against it, and waited just a few feet from the door.

Another creak. The man was outside her bedroom. The pounding of her heart deafened her. She sucked in a breath and tightened her grip on the lamp.

The handle turned and the door pushed open.

A hand fumbled on the wall, flicked the switch, and the room flooded with light.

A gasp slipped from Shelly's mouth. The person standing before her was not Scott Bilow.

"Lucy."

Lucy looked momentarily stunned that Shelly was standing and was not asleep in her bed. In an instant, her expression changed from surprise to pure hate.

"It would have been easier for you if you stayed asleep." The words rasped from Lucy's throat. "It will be worse for you now." Her fists clenched into tight balls.

"What are you doing, Lucy?" Shelly wanted to get the woman talking in order to buy time.

"You know what I'm doing." Lucy glanced at the lamp in Shelly's hand.

"Why? Why are you doing this?"

Lucy's eyes darkened with rage. "You know why," she seethed. "He belongs to me."

"Jack?"

"Yes, Jack." The words came out like a hiss.

"I'm not dating Jack," Shelly said. "We're friends."

"We're just friends." Lucy said the words in a mocking, sing-song way. She said the sentence three times and the weird repetition made Shelly's blood run cold.

Shelly listened for a police siren hoping Juliet had seen her text. She cursed herself for not calling 911 on her own and for not trying to go out the window before Lucy found her.

"Did you date Jack?" Shelly questioned.

"He belongs to me. He's not yours. He didn't belong to Meg or Jill either." Little beads of sweat showed on Lucy's forehead and her blond hair was disheveled and hung over her eyes. She took a step forward, her eyes on Shelly like lasers. "You couldn't have just stayed asleep, could you?"

Shelly tried to swallow the fear lodged in her throat. "You caught the other two women unaware. I'm fully awake." She swung the lamp at her side like a Billy club.

Lucy released a cackle. Her haughty, ugly smile contorted into a sneer. "I have a black belt in mixed martial arts."

"And I'm ready to fight you to the death," Shelly whispered.

Justice leapt from under the bed to the window and dug her claws into the screen trying to climb to the top. The spilt-second distraction was enough. Shelly charged at the woman swinging the lamp base. It connected with Lucy's shoulder and knocked her to her knees.

Shelly ran from the room, down the hall, into the kitchen. Fumbling with the door, she heard Lucy's feet pounding on the floor towards her. In seconds, the backdoor flew open, but Lucy lunged at Shelly and the two crashed down the three steps to the ground.

They rolled, threw punches, kicked. Each time Lucy attempted to wrap her fingers around Shelly's neck, Shelly managed to heave her body to the side and throw the woman off.

Lucy was fiercely strong. Shelly knew she wouldn't be able to keep her at bay much longer.

Straddling Shelly, Lucy wrapped her fingers around the young woman's neck like a vise.

Unable to suck in any air, Shelly's eyes bugged. She bucked and thrashed. Staring up at the stars, she could feel herself fading. It wouldn't be long. Soon it would all go black.

A scream pierced the air. Someone leapt onto Lucy's back and threw her off balance causing her hands to pull away from Shelly's throat.

A horrible sucking sound filled the air as Shelly wheezed and pulled precious oxygen into her lungs.

Juliet pummeled Lucy in the head before being

flipped over onto her back by the powerful woman. Lucy growled like a wild animal and got in two punches to Juliet's face before Shelly was on the woman to launch her own pounding attack.

While Shelly and Lucy battled, Juliet, panting, crawled over the grass to the patio, lifted the loose brick, and pushed her battered body up.

With a maniacal look on her face, Lucy had Shelly pinned again and was choking the life out of her.

Juliet darted up behind them and with a hard, quick motion, smashed the brick down on top of Lucy's head. Lucy swayed for a moment and then keeled to the side.

Shelly rolled to her knees, coughing, spitting, and gasping.

A police siren wailed.

"Now they show up," Juliet muttered holding tight to the brick in case Lucy made another move.

Justice dashed to her owner, put both front paws on Shelly's leg, and trilled.

24

L ucy Millhouse was arrested for breaking and entering and for assault and battery and was at the hospital undergoing a psychiatric evaluation. There was no doubt in anyone's mind that she would also soon be charged with the murders of Meg Stores and Jill Murray.

Shelly and Juliet sat in the warm sun on lounge chairs outside on the patio where not long ago they had fought Lucy Millhouse for their lives. Justice snoozed, curled up on Shelly's stomach.

Shelly had a splint on one of her fingers that broke in the attack and she also suffered two cracked ribs. She and Juliet looked like twins, both with bruises, cuts, scrapes, and black eyes. Juliet's nose, although not broken, was swollen from her taking multiple hits in the face. They each had strained their backs and now walked hunched over like they'd been run over by buses.

"As long as I don't move," Juliet said, "I don't feel bad at all."

Shelly started to chuckle, but the pain in her side changed the laugh to a groan of pain. "Don't say anything funny. Never again."

Juliet sipped from her glass of lemonade. "Let's milk this for a couple of weeks."

"I don't think I have to pretend about injuries. I'll barely be able to crawl back into the diner in two weeks."

"You know what?" Juliet leaned against the chair and looked up at the puffy clouds lazily moving across the bright blue sky. "I'm proud of us. We did good."

Shelly turned her head and smiled. "We sure did." Running her hand over the cat's warm, soft fur, she added, "And this kitty did pretty well, too. If she hadn't heard Lucy break into the house, well, who knows what would have happened if Justice didn't wake me." They all knew very well what would have happened and what the outcome probably would have been, but they left that horror unsaid.

Justice had run from the house when Shelly and Lucy fell out the door on the night of the attack. The cat howled outside Juliet's window until she woke up. Seeing the cat and hearing the fight behind Shelly's house, Juliet called the police and tore into the yard. Thinking things through afterwards, she'd wished she's grabbed her pepper spray and a weapon before dashing to join the melee.

"All's well that ends well," Shelly had told her friend even though she had her own misgivings about how she'd handled the break-in and attack.

Juliet nodded. "Next time, we'll do even better."

"There better not be a next time," Shelly groaned hoping that these additional injuries wouldn't greatly impact the recovery that had been underway from the car accident. "I've had enough bodily injury over these past months."

"What we need is a week on a Caribbean island."

"Only if we can bring the cat."

Lucy Millhouse's obsession with Jack Graham had caused the deaths of two young women, and nearly a third one. She had dated Jack a few times when he had moved to Paxton Park, but Jack chose not to continue seeing the woman. Lucy did not take that news well. She stalked Jack, called him incessantly, showed up outside his house. When he started to date Meg Stores, Lucy's harassment of Jack stopped and her focus became fixed on Meg. One night when she'd met friends at the resort pub, Meg's car wouldn't start. Lucy offered her a lift, drove to an isolated spot in the forest and strangled Meg, dumping her body not far from the crooked trees.

Lucy then fixated on Jill Murray when she saw the woman's interaction with Jack at the pub one night. She followed the woman and bided her time. Lucy attacked when Jill went running on the mountain trails.

Shelly was next.

As it turned out, Maria Stores had indeed spent down Meg's inheritance and was preparing to flee the country with what remained so that her sister wouldn't be able to get her hands on it. When Maria met Scott Bilow and learned of his financial problems, she hatched a plan to involve him in the inheritance scandal hoping to push blame for the misuse of funds onto him.

"Two awful people," Juliet had declared. "They both deserved to be punished. Maria for stealing her sister's money and Scott for being a bumbling, harassing monster."

The threatening note that Maria found in Meg's files had been written by Lucy. One night at dinner with a group of people they both knew, Lucy carefully dropped the note in Meg's open purse when she went to the restroom. Although Lucy hadn't confessed to it yet, the police believed that she was responsible for setting the fire at Meg's rented house, either to get rid of the note or in another irrational surge of rage against the dead woman.

One day shortly after the attack, Shelly was sitting in the rocking chair on the front porch when Jack Graham drove up and parked in front of the house. He emerged from his vehicle carrying a vase of wildflowers.

"Excuse me," Jack said with a twinkle in his eye. "Does a Michelle Taylor live at this house?"

Shelly answered, "What's left of her does."

Jack laughed and climbed the steps to hand her the vase of colorful flowers.

"They're beautiful." Shelly smiled, wishing she didn't look like such an ugly brawl victim covered in bruises.

"I picked the flowers from the field we biked by the other day. I hoped they'd remind you of what a nice time we had ... and how you promised to bike with me again."

"I'd love to bike again. We're just going to have to push the day off a couple of weeks until I can actually move again."

"I'm a patient man." Jack grinned.

The two talked about Lucy Millhouse and how adept she could be at hiding her obsession. Jack expressed guilt for being the object of the woman's infatuation, not recognizing how far she would take it, and for the deaths of Meg and Jill.

Shelly said gently, "You know you aren't to blame. Lucy was ill. Her illness was the cause, not you."

"Logically, I know that." Jack rubbed at the back of his neck. "Emotionally, well, that's another story."

Justice jumped onto the man's lap, put her paws on his chest, and touched her nose to his. Jack's laugh lit up the space.

Shelly looked at the sweet animal settling on Jack's lap. "Justice says that nothing about the mess was your fault."

"Okay, kitty." Jack patted the calico. "I'll try and hold onto that."

After rocking and chatting for another hour, Jack announced that he was starving. "How about I go to Chet's Market, pick up some food, and come back and cook dinner for both of us."

Shelly started to protest, but Jack cut her off. "We're both hungry. We're having a nice time ... at least, I am. I like to cook and you're in no shape to prepare a meal. It's win-win."

"Okay, as long as I get to cook for you when I'm feeling better." Shelly's eyes glimmered.

Jack was back in a flash with two grocery bags in his arms. "I didn't think you could drink alcohol while you're on pain killers so I picked up a bottle of sparkling pear juice. We can pretend it's champagne." He helped Shelly into the kitchen and told her to supervise from the kitchen chair. Putting on some music, Jack sang as he made the dinner, even throwing a bit of dancing into his performance to make Shelly laugh. In a short time, he'd made a tossed salad, grilled broccoli, rice, and baked salmon. Jack winked. "I picked fish for the meal so that Justice would like it, too."

He slid open the wide kitchen doors to let in the evening breeze, lit some candles and placed them on the center of the table, and served the food.

"This is wonderful," Shelly announced more than once.

Justice gobbled up her portion and sat back washing her face with her paw.

After they ate, Jack settled Shelly on the sofa with pillows behind her back and a cup of tea on the side table and then he cleaned up the dishes. He put the vase of wildflowers on the coffee table and then they watched a movie together.

In the middle of the film's scary part, Jack reached over and held Shelly's hand and when he did that, warmth spread through her body, and surprisingly, her bruises and breaks didn't hurt quite as much anymore.

THANK YOU FOR READING!

BOOKS BY J.A. WHITING

To hear about new books and book sales, please sign up for my mailing list at:

www.jawhitingbooks.com

Your email will never be sold, shared, or spammed.

If you enjoyed the book, please consider leaving a review. A few words are all that's needed. It would be very much appreciated.

BOOK SERIES BY J. A. WHITING

PAXTON PARK COZY MYSTERIES

CLAIRE ROLLINS COZY MYSTERIES

LIN COFFIN COZY MYSTERIES

SWEET COVE COZY MYSTERIES

OLIVIA MILLER MYSTERIES (not cozy)

ABOUT THE AUTHOR

J.A. Whiting lives with her family in New England. Whiting loves reading and writing mystery stories.

Visit me at:

www.jawhitingbooks.com/

www.facebook.com/jawhitingauthor

66681027R00142

Made in the USA
Middletown, DE
14 March 2018